PRAISE FOR BARRY FORBES AND THE MYSTERY SEARCHERS FAMILY BOOK SERIES

AMAZING BOOK! My daughter is in 6th grade and she is homeschooled, she really enjoyed reading this book. Highly recommend to middle schoolers. *Rubi Pizarro on Amazon*

I have three boys 11-15 and finding a book they all like is sometimes a challenge This series is great! My 15-year-old said, "I actually like it better than Hardy Boys because it tells me currents laws about technology that I didn't know." My reluctant 13-year-old picked it up without any prodding and that's not an easy feat. *Shantelshomeschool on Instagram*

I stumbled across the author and his series on Instagram and had to order the first book! Fun characters, good storyline too, easy reading. Best for ages 11 and up. *AZmommy2011 on Amazon*

Virtues of kindness, leadership, compassion, responsibility, loyalty, courage, diligence, perseverance, loyalty and service are characterized throughout the book. *Lynn G. on Amazon*

Barry, he LOVED it! My son is almost 14 and enjoys reading but most books are historical fiction or non-fiction. He carried your book everywhere, reading in any spare moments. He can't wait for book 2 – I'm ordering today and book 3 for his birthday. *Ourlifeathome on Instagram*

Perfect series for our 7th grader! I'm thrilled to have come across this perfect series for my 13-year old son this summer. We purchased the entire set! They are easy, but captivating reads and he is enjoying them very much. *Amyl-carney on Amazon*

Great "clean" page turner! My son was hooked after the first three chapters and kept asking me to read more... Fast forward three hours and we were done! When you read a book in one sitting, you know it is a good one. *Homework and Horseplay on Amazon*

"Great book for kids and no worry for parents! I bought and read this book with my grandson in mind. What a great book! The plot was well done using the sleuths' knowledge of modern technology to solve this mystery." *Regina Krause on Amazon*

"Take a break, wander away from the real world into the adventurous life of spunky kids out to save the world in the hidden hills of the Southwest." *Ron Boat on Amazon*

"Books so engaging my teenager woke up early and stayed up late to finish the story. After the first book, he asked: Are there more in this series? We HAVE to get them! He even chipped in some cash to buy more books." *Sabrinakaadven-tures on Instagram*

THE CRYPTIC CODE ON DEAD MAN'S PASS

A MYSTERY SEARCHERS BOOK

BARRY FORBES

THE CRYPTIC CODE ON DEAD MAN'S PASS

A MYSTERY SEARCHERS BOOK

Volume 12

For Linda,
whose steadfast love and encouragement
made this series possible

DISCLAIMER

Prescott, the former capital of the Arizona Territory, is considered by many to be the state's crown jewel. Aside from this Central Arizona locale, *The Mystery Searchers Family Book Series* is a work of fiction. Names, characters, businesses, places, events, incidents, and other locales are either the products of the author's imagination or used in a fictitious manner. Any resemblance to actual persons, living or dead, or actual events is purely coincidental.

Read more at www.MysterySearchers.com.

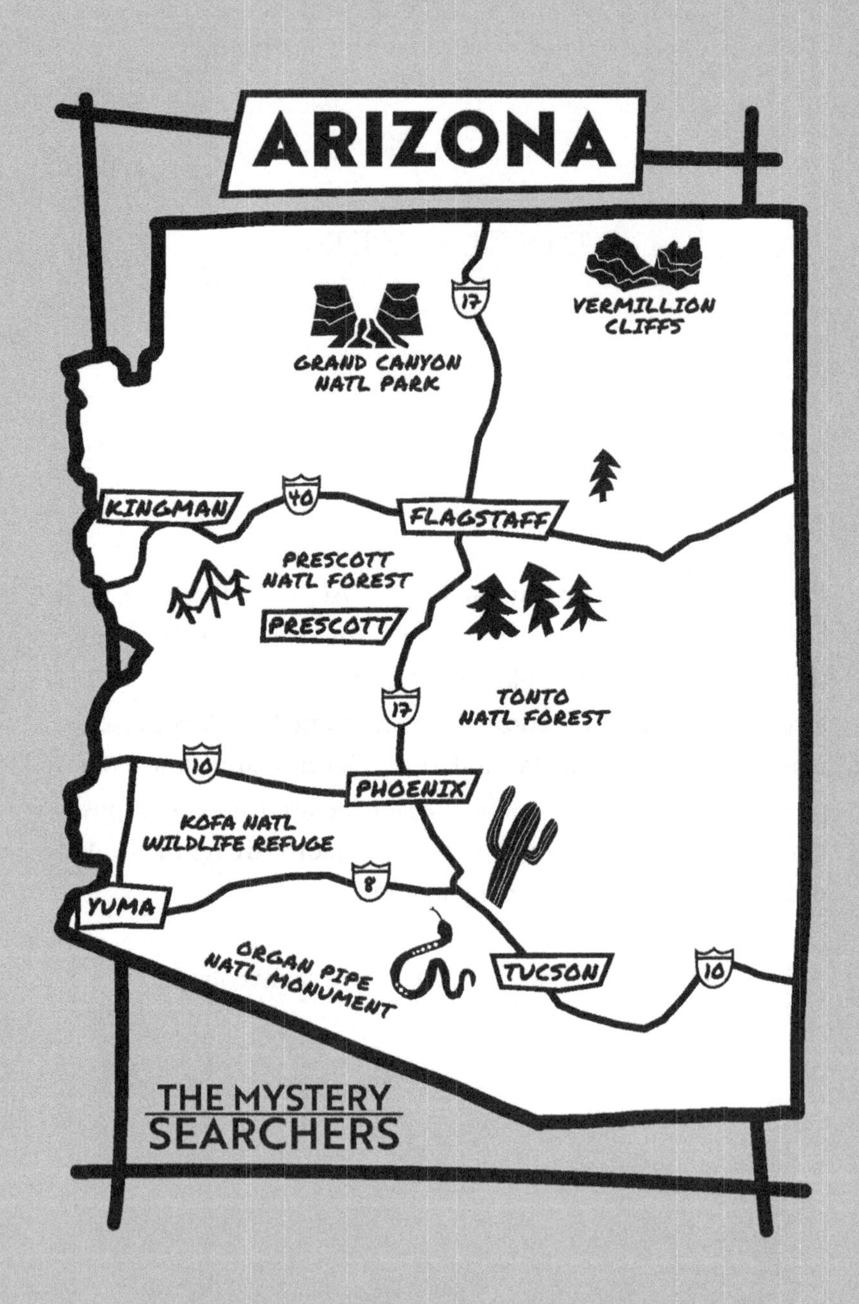
ARIZONA
VERMILLION CLIFFS
GRAND CANYON NATL PARK
17
KINGMAN
40
FLAGSTAFF
PRESCOTT NATL FOREST
PRESCOTT
17
TONTO NATL FOREST
10
PHOENIX
KOFA NATL WILDLIFE REFUGE
8
YUMA
ORGAN PIPE NATL MONUMENT
TUCSON
10
THE MYSTERY SEARCHERS

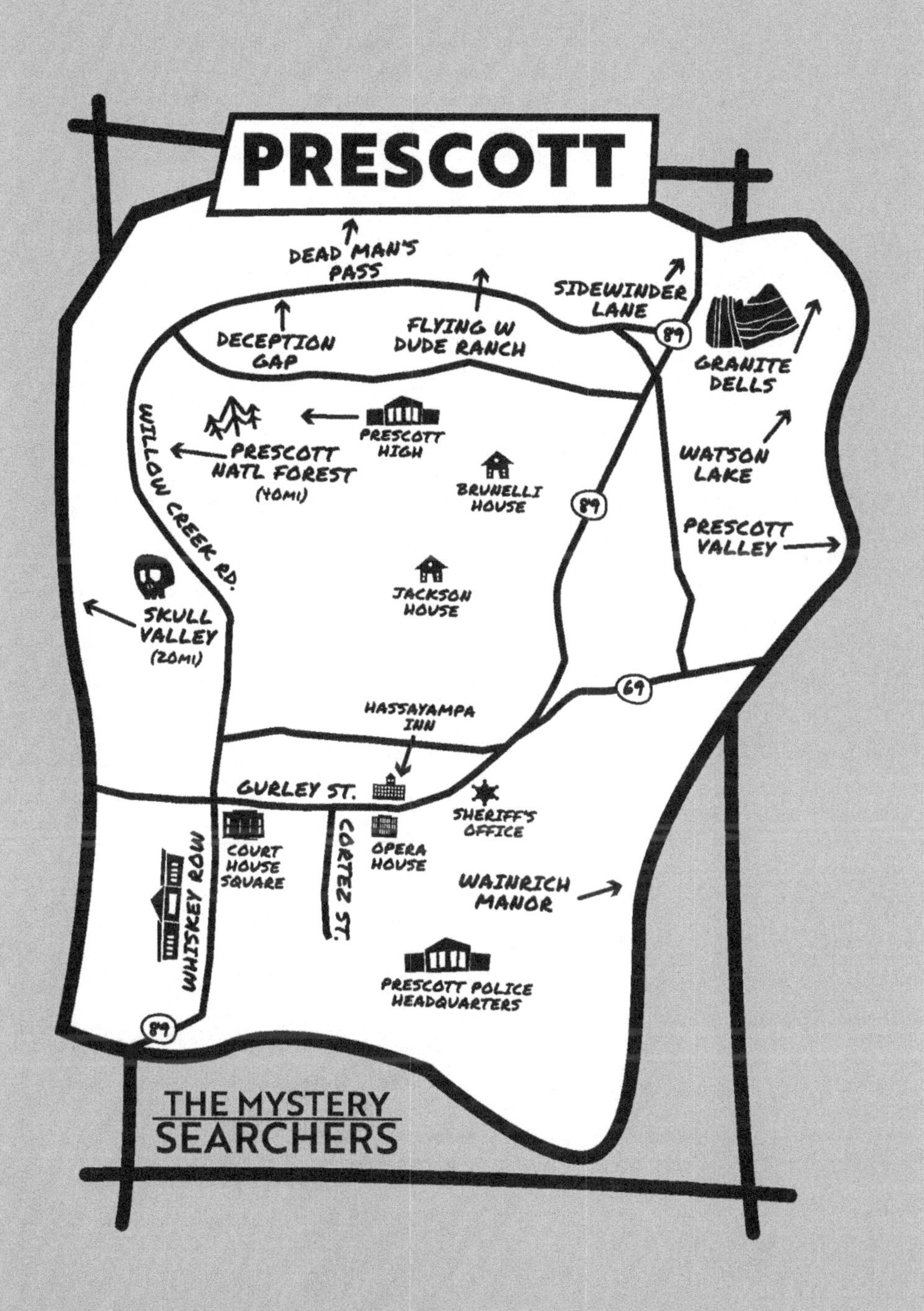
PRESCOTT
DEAD MAN'S PASS
SIDEWINDER LANE
DECEPTION GAP
FLYING W DUDE RANCH
89
GRANITE DELLS
PRESCOTT HIGH
WILLOW CREEK RD.
PRESCOTT NATL FOREST (40MI)
BRUNELLI HOUSE
WATSON LAKE
89
PRESCOTT VALLEY
JACKSON HOUSE
SKULL VALLEY (20MI)
69
HASSAYAMPA INN
GURLEY ST.
SHERIFF'S OFFICE
COURT HOUSE SQUARE
CORTEZ ST.
OPERA HOUSE
WHISKEY ROW
WAINRICH MANOR
PRESCOTT POLICE HEADQUARTERS
89
THE MYSTERY SEARCHERS

1

A MIDNIGHT HIKE

Dense fog had rolled in earlier on New Year's Eve. The insidious gray mist, cold and clammy, had gathered in the rugged low-lying country around the trailhead that led up to Dead Man's Pass, deep in the canyon-riddled badlands north of Prescott, Arizona. As the hours ticked by, the fog had risen higher and higher and grown thicker and thicker, seemingly unstoppable. Now, just past midnight on New Year's Day, it had seeped all the way to the upper reaches of the trail, enveloping Kathy Brunelli in an icy grip.

She paused to catch her breath. The steady upward-sloping hike had taken its toll. She thrust her flashlight ahead, lighting a narrow cone of . . . fog. Kathy shivered—the kind of shiver that no one likes, reaching from her throat all the way down to her toes. Even with her warm hiking boots and a double layer of socks, her feet felt like blocks of ice. Not surprising, really. The temperature had continued to fall and, sure enough, a gentle snow shower now began sifting down from the black sky, turning the rocky trail into a slippery hazard. Fog plus snow: white on white.

"Why am I even here?" Kathy grumbled out loud, knowing no one was within hearing distance. *Just venting,* she thought glumly. Her brother, Pete, had raced ahead and vanished somewhere in the fog. Their friend Heidi Hoover was even farther up the trail.

From Kathy's perspective, the situation had grown worse with every passing minute. The awful, almost impenetrable white mist had blotted out everything near and far, even before the silent snowfall. *Not good.* Plus, every sluggish step forward pushed them higher along the increasingly treacherous trail.

"Creeps me right out," Kathy whispered to herself. "What a way to spend New Year's Eve! I can't believe it."

To her left rose a towering wall of rock, perhaps ten stories high or higher. "Keep one hand on the wall at all times," Heidi Hoover had reminded the siblings earlier. "Let it be your guide. If you don't . . ." She didn't finish. Why? Because five feet to the right was a sheer drop to the canyon floor. A long, *long* way straight down.

Heidi also mentioned the many deep coves, natural weathered carveouts that punctured the face of the granite wall. "Keep track of them. If you think someone's coming, duck back into the last one you passed. They can't spot you in there. Too dark."

"They" who? No one had a clue.

Another five minutes of strenuous hiking ensued before Kathy dared raise her voice. "Pete," she hissed. No answer. *"Pete!"*

From somewhere ahead came a leaden response. "What?"

"I'm not liking this."

"What else is new?"

"I can't see a thing. Where's Heidi?"

"*Sssh!* She's up front. You worry too much."

"You don't worry enough."

Silence descended around Kathy once more, broken by nothing but her own footfalls and sharp gasps. *Oh, Lord,* a voice pleaded within her. *How do we get into these predicaments? What're Suzanne and Tom doing right now? Lucky ducks, they won the toss. Why did I agree to this . . . this . . . ?*

But she knew, of course. The person responsible for their wintery trek was none other than Heidi Hoover herself, their good friend and *The Daily Pilot's* star reporter. Heidi had often featured the Brunellis and their best friends and fellow sleuths, Tom and Suzanne—the Jackson twins—on the front page of Prescott's hometown newspaper. It was Heidi who had dubbed the four friends "the mystery searchers" after their first case. The moniker had stuck. It had not taken long for Heidi to become a mystery searcher in her own right.

"We *could* blame the anonymous joker who mailed that weird poem," Kathy murmured quietly. That's what set them off on this freezing-cold wild goose chase. Three nights earlier, in fact. That's when Heidi had first messaged them. The foursome was on Christmas break from Prescott High, with ten days' vacation left to go. Perfect timing for a new case. But this—*this*—was something Kathy hadn't counted on. *Oh, well,* she brooded. *It'll soon be over. And the sooner, the—*

"Hide, Kathy!" Pete's voice rasped. *"I'm hiding too! Someone's coming."*

His sister spun around and quickly retraced her steps. She ran her right hand along the rock wall, her heart racing. The last cove was fifty yards farther back, give or take, she guessed.

There. Ducking in, Kathy shrank down and squeezed into a corner and doused her flashlight. As adrenaline coursed through her veins, she forgot about her frozen feet and stared, transfixed, at the wall of mist beyond the cove's opening.

A woman screamed!

Oh, Lord, that's gotta be Heidi, Kathy thought. *What just happened?*

A minute slipped by before the sound of stumbling feet caught her attention. A man cursed in a loud voice. Three figures hustled past in single file, so close that Kathy heard their breath coming in gasps. Each silhouetted, fog-shrouded figure was carrying . . . something. *Now what?* More time passed before a fourth figure—a familiar shape—shot past, empty-handed.

"Pete!" she called out softly.

No answer, nor did he glance her way.

Oh, my goodness. He didn't even hear me. Kathy jumped to her feet and peeked around the edge of the cove's entrance. Nothing but fog. Heidi must be somewhere up ahead—in trouble. Kathy turned left, gliding the fingertips of her left hand along the wall as she headed higher. She switched her flashlight back on and probed the mist ahead. Two anxious minutes passed before the star reporter emerged, sitting on a boulder, clutching her knees, and nursing a nasty head wound. Kathy saw drops of blood on the snow at Heidi's feet. *Argh . . .*

"Heidi, are you okay?"

"Define *okay,*" she replied, wincing. "At the present time, my pride hurts the most."

"What happened?"

"Remember when I said they'd never look in the coves?"

"Sure."

"Well, I didn't take the possibility of flashlights into consideration. We have them, so why wouldn't they? Some guy clicked one on and pointed it into my hiding place.

Then he stepped in, stooped down, and decked me with it."

"Decked you? With his flashlight!" Kathy fell to one knee. "Are you . . . still bleeding?" Just the thought of blood panicked her. And snakes too, of course. Blood and serpents: Kathy's top two phobias. Her *only* phobias.

"Not so much. Pete donated his handkerchief after those evil dudes took off. He hid from them, then raced up to help me. But I'll tell you something: it was worth it."

"Worth it?" Kathy stared at her friend in disbelief. "What do you mean?"

Heidi's voice turned oddly low and guttural. "I glared right back into the guy's eyes, just inches away. And before this is over, I'm gonna plant his mug on the front page of *The Daily Pilot!*"

"Good for you," Kathy said. "Whoever he is, he deserves it. Are you okay to walk down?"

"You're kidding, right?" Heidi struggled to her feet. "We haven't reached our goal. Not even close." She turned up the trail. "Follow me. We've gotta figure out where those creeps came from."

Kathy coughed. *Oh, joy.*

MEANWHILE, WORRY HAD WORMED ITS WAY—uncharacteristically—into Pete's mind. Down at the trailhead, he knew, the Jackson twins waited. Tom and Suzanne had settled for the anchor position when the foursome flipped coins to divvy up tasks for the night's adventure. The way Pete looked at it, the twins had lost. They hid their Chevy in a clump of leafless willows and stayed behind, guarding the Dead Man's Pass trailhead.

"If the bad guys come down, you'll be here, watching for

them," Heidi had instructed. "Make sure they don't spot you. I'd say get some phone pix, but with this fog . . ."

"That makes no sense," Tom argued. "The only vehicle out here is ours. How could anyone escape?"

"Maybe someone picks them up," Suzanne thought aloud.

"I don't have answers," Heidi countered. "Not yet anyway. But I'll tell you something. On the second night when I was here before, my car was the only one around. Two men passed me on the trail, heading down. I tracked them, but by the time I reached the bottom they had vanished into thin air. No way could I figure out where. Or how."

Pete grunted. "Not gonna happen on my watch, guaranteed!"

Now, just hours later, *three* men were heading to the canyon floor. Pete pressed ahead, one hand gliding along the rock wall, doing his best not to slip. Twice he stopped dead in his tracks, listening. *Yes.* Impossible to see the men, but their footfalls gave them away. Someone sneezed, a sound instantly swallowed by the fog and snow in the normally echoey pass. The men still enjoyed a slim lead.

Minutes later, Pete paused for a third time. Something had changed. No sound anywhere now. *Nothing.* So they'd reached the trailhead, right? Close to the trailhead himself now, Pete picked up his pace. Soon, the trail leveled out as he hustled out onto the canyon floor and crossed over toward the willows. It was too foggy to see a thing. *"Tom! Suzanne!"* he called softly.

"We're here!" Suzanne yelled from behind a giant willow. "Coming your way."

Whew. "Did you spot them?" Pete shouted back. "The three men? What were they hauling out of here?"

The twins materialized from the gray mist. "Three men?" Tom said. "No way. Just us, the whole time."

"Where're Kathy and Heidi?" Suzanne asked, wide-eyed.

"Still up there," Pete replied. "You didn't see *anyone* coming off the trail?"

Tom shook his head. "Nope. Not a soul. What happened?"

"How far up are they?" Suzanne asked.

"Okay, so now I'm freaked right out," Pete said, ignoring his friends. "There's a single trail up and down. And you're telling me three bad dudes just disappeared off the face of the planet." He paused, struggling to connect the dots. "Who are they? What were they doing up there? *And where'd they go?*"

2

THREE DAYS EARLIER

On Thursday, December twenty-seventh, shortly after 9:00 a.m., the mail arrived at *The Daily Pilot,* Prescott's hometown newspaper. The uniformed delivery person, a youngish woman with a cheerful disposition named Constance—most people at the *Pilot* called her Connie—greeted Betsy, the receptionist, with a friendly wave and dropped a foot-high stack of mail onto the counter. Then she turned and pushed open the front door.

"You have a nice day," Constance called out before stepping back into the wintery weather.

Prescott—sometimes called Arizona's Christmas City—sits in the center of the state, nestled in a mile-high basin among pine-dotted mountains. In December, a few inches of snow often transforms the city into a chilly winter wonderland.

"Thanks, Connie!" Betsy sang out. "Make sure you stay warm out there!"

Betsy sorted through the pile, dumping most of it into a rectangular blue recycling bin beside her desk: junk mail.

She routed checks and bills to accounting, everything else to the business office. Everything, that is, except for one envelope addressed to Heidi Hoover. "World's Best Reporter" someone had written in flowing letters beneath the ZIP code. Betsy grinned before depositing the envelope onto the star reporter's desk. *Definitely Prescott's best reporter!* she thought.

That day and the next, Heidi chased breaking stories for the *Pilot*'s weekend edition. She failed to even glance at the envelope until late Friday afternoon. What caught her attention was that notation below the address: "World's Best Reporter." A smile crossed her face. The letter had been postmarked a day earlier at Prescott's main post office, only two blocks away. To Heidi, the handwriting—with its flowing, precise cursive—suggested that a woman had addressed the letter. A teacher, or perhaps a librarian. Or a calligrapher! *Beautiful.*

Heidi pried open the back flap and withdrew a single sheet of paper, folded once. Opening it, she was surprised to see that someone had typed out a rhyming quatrain—a four-line poem. It read:

> *Search for a crime on Dead Man's Pass,*
> *A secret run at the midnight hour.*
> *But beware of a dangerous few,*
> *Engaged beside the granite tower.*

That certainly intrigued her. Everything about the letter, in fact. *Big time.* She stared at the poem, studying each line, reading it silently again and again. *What to do?* "It's a hoax," Heidi mumbled to herself. "Doesn't mean a thing."

But somehow that conclusion didn't hold up under further scrutiny. *Why would someone even bother?* Maybe it wasn't a hoax at all. Although a little letter is an easy thing to write. And yet . . .

If it *was* genuine, an unknown individual had sent her a message in code—a cryptic code, to be sure. But why? And why her? One thing everyone knew about Heidi: the diminutive reporter didn't give up easily and never shied away from a promising story, no matter how implausible it might seem. If a crime really had been committed by "a dangerous few" out in Dead Man's Pass, and if she could uncover the story, it might well land on the front page—a place Heidi definitely liked her work to be. The anonymous quatrain writer was obviously aware of Heidi's reputation—admired her even.

Maybe the letter was a lead. Maybe. *But what did it mean?* Heidi had hiked the pass—twice, with her close friends, the mystery searchers. It was quite a drive out and a long walk to get there: North on Highway 87, then way, *way* off the highway, halfway to Sedona. Dead Man's Pass is all but hidden in Arizona's badlands—rough, unforgiving country, with just a single daunting trail all the way to the summit. It is a hard, rugged climb, not for the faint-hearted.

The hiking trail rises steeply from the get-go, beginning at the marked trailhead down in the badlands. For the first few hundred yards or so, the path is flanked on the left by towering boulders, many of them several stories high, some split by dramatic fissures. Through the narrow gaps, hikers can glimpse a steeply sloping field of jagged rocks that looks simply impassible. The boulders gradually cohere into a towering rock wall that continues on hikers' left side all the way up, and on their right coming down

As Heidi remembered well from prior experience, the hiking trail is challenging all the way up. Opposite the looming cliff face on one side is a sheer descending cliff on the other. One misstep and a hiker could be in deep trouble.

It's a *long* way to the bottom—and longer the higher up the trail you go. Which is where the name of the pass came from. Say it out loud and your mouth runs dry.

"A crime?" It was hard to imagine what crime anyone would want to commit up there. There was nothing to steal —it was rocks and more rocks. Nary even a single tree. "A secret run at the midnight hour?" Heidi smiled, her eyebrows arching. She knew what had to be done. In a sudden rush, she grabbed her cellphone and captured a quick shot of the cryptic quatrain, and a second pic of the envelope, with its address in flowing cursive.

Then she headed home to pick up a few things.

3

NO GO

That same evening, the mystery searchers had taken in a late movie at the mall. Afterward, they made their way back to the Jacksons' Chevy under the harsh, misted glare of the parking lot lights, prodded by a biting wind.

"Man, talk about action and adventure," Pete said with a note of satisfaction. "Great show!"

"It was just okay," his sister countered.

Pete groaned. "You can't be serious."

That caused the twins to chuckle. The Brunellis bickered often, but they cared deeply about each other too.

Anyone glancing at the foursome would have seen two sets of siblings who couldn't have appeared more different if they tried. The Brunellis were Italian through and through, a trifle shorter and stockier than their best friends, with coal-black hair and olive-hued skin. They looked alike to be mistaken for twins. Not as much as the Jacksons, who, after all, really were twins—both tall and willowy, with fair skin and dark-blond hair.

As the foursome dove into the Chevy, Suzanne reached

for her cellphone and checked for messages. "Text from Heidi," she said.

"What's up?" Kathy asked.

"The message says, 'Look what arrived in the mail. See you soon.' And she attached two images. Let's see . . . Whoa!"

"Whoa what?" Pete asked.

"Manners," his sister admonished.

"Check this out," Suzanne said. "Heidi received an anonymous letter at the newspaper." She enlarged the image. "Just four lines. It's a little poem. I'll read it out loud: 'Search for a crime on Dead Man's Pass, / A secret run at the midnight hour. / But beware of a dangerous few, / Engaged beside the granite tower.'"

Suzanne's brother, Tom, was at the wheel. "Dead Man's Pass . . . we hiked out there more than once. Remember how rugged it was?"

"It's a long way to the top, bro," Pete recalled. "Serious hiking, for sure."

"Freaks you right out," Kathy said. "Coming down was just as bad as going up. People have fallen off that trail, right? All the way to the bottom. That's where the name came from." She shuddered at the thought. "And in winter? No thanks."

Pete shot a certain look her way. "Best hike ever."

"It's a quatrain," Suzanne said, thinking out loud. "A four-line poem. This one rhymes. But what does it mean?"

"Well," Tom deduced, "it's pointing to a crime that's taking place out there. Around midnight. Sounds like whatever's happening is somewhere along the trail."

"So 'granite tower' just means the canyon walls?" Suzanne asked. "I'm not sure that rock is really granite."

"A crime?" Kathy asked, then responded immediately to

her own question. "There's nothing out there. I mean *nothing*. Just rocks, heat, scorpions, and snakes."

In Pete's world, the very thought of something dangerous was like waving a red flag at a bull. Unless it involved tight spaces. Pete was kind of claustrophobic. He tweaked his sister. "Uh, you do realize it's wintertime, right? Nothing to worry about in the rocks-heat-scorpions-snakes department..."

"Everything's fine," Kathy parried, "unless you fall off the trail."

"The message could be fake," Tom said soberly. "A hoax."

"There's another attachment," Suzanne said. "Okay, it's the envelope addressed to Heidi. Whoever wrote it added, 'World's Best Reporter' under the ZIP code. One of her fans —with a woman's handwriting, looks like. Beautiful, flowing cursive."

"There's nothing like a woman scorned," Pete said, smirking.

Kathy glared at her brother. "You don't know that. You don't know anything yet."

"Just saying," Pete replied flippantly. "Let's call Heidi."

Suzanne checked the time. "It's awfully late."

"No problem," Tom said, reaching for his cellphone. "That girl's a night owl." He touched Heidi's name and went straight to an outgoing message:

"Hi, you've reached Heidi Hoover. I'll be hiking this weekend in an area without phone service. Leave your name and number and I'll get back to you on Sunday night. Bye!

The mystery searchers glanced at one another with knowing eyes. "She's already out there," Tom said, almost reverently. Heidi never failed to amaze him.

"Yup," Pete said, loving it. "Dead Man's Pass."

"Alone?" Suzanne exclaimed, aghast. "On a winter night?"

Kathy blinked. "That's not good."

Pete sucked in air. "Sounds like a blast to me. Let's go!"

"If Heidi wanted us there, she'd have asked," Suzanne said pointedly. "But she didn't."

"But—but she just told us where she was," Pete argued. "I mean, c'mon! She might need our help."

"She can take care of herself," Kathy hurried to add.

"Tom, what do you think?" his sister asked.

"Her cellphone won't work out there. My guess is she'll return home tonight, then head back tomorrow. Let's call her every hour or two, starting first thing in the morning. Maybe we can help."

Pete shrugged. "You guys have no sense of adventure," he muttered.

4

A LONELY MISSION

A line of willow trees, set into a deep-seated gully, bordered the parking area at the Dead Man's Pass trailhead. Heidi circled in behind the trees and cut her lights, screening her two-door sports car from the view of any passing vehicle. Not that she was at all concerned; there had been zero traffic on the thirty-mile journey along the gravel road. *Who's to worry?*

Heidi glanced at her cellphone: no bars, no service. She felt grateful that she had messaged Suzanne earlier. Someone needed to know her location. Why? One word from the quatrain replayed in her mind: 'dangerous.' Whatever that meant, she couldn't be too careful.

She checked the time: 10:00 p.m. *Great.* That gave her about a two-hour window on either side of the "midnight hour" that the poem has mentioned to hike halfway up to the summit before bedding down at a late but decent hour. There she planned to crash in one of the natural carveouts that punctuated the stone wall on one side of the trail. If she didn't spot anyone, she'd continue up on Saturday morning, then bunk down up top that same evening.

Heidi stepped into the freezing cold night and pulled on a heavy fleece-lined insulated jacket, warm as toast. She had prepared well, including lined pants and water-resistant hiking boots. The first thing that struck her—something she hadn't even considered—was the high fogbank hugging the canyon floor. No problem. She reached into her trunk and grabbed a backpack stocked with water, food, and emergency supplies, and her sleeping bag and a self-inflating sleeping mat, both secured on the outside with straps. She slung the pack over her shoulders and secured the waist and chest straps. Then she locked up her car and headed into the pitch-black wilderness, sweeping her flashlight ahead to keep to the trail.

It wasn't until one o'clock on Saturday morning that Heidi rolled out her thermal sleeping bag—rated for temperatures down to −10 degrees Fahrenheit—and bunked down in a cozy cove. Exhausted after the long, steep climb, she fell into a deep sleep.

A RISING SUN AND SCREECHING BIRDS AWOKE HEIDI EARLY. Two hawks soared high above, putting on quite a show over the pass. Well-rested despite the hard ground she had slept on—thanks to her hi-tech camping mat—and eager to take on the day, she drank a measured portion of her water, conserving some for later. Her backup, she knew, was melted snow. After consuming four energy bars, she repacked her gear, shouldered her backpack, and started up the rough trail.

Heid's mind replayed the second line of the quatrain: "A secret run at the midnight hour." Doubts had filtered up out of her subconscious mind, but she knew one thing for sure: If the "dangerous few" really existed, they couldn't possibly traverse the pass *every* night.

At one point on her way up, Heidi noticed boot prints in a thin layer of old snow. Since it had snowed the day after Christmas, that meant people—two, it appeared from the prints—had hiked Dead Man's Pass about twenty-four hours earlier. *Before I arrived last evening. And whoever they are, their tracks seem to go only one way. They're still up there!*

Nothing unusual about that. Although the pass was off the beaten path, it did attract serious hikers and campers. *But there's only one car at the trailhead,* she thought. *Mine.*

Heidi followed the same boot prints up the trail, wherever they appeared in the thin crust of snow. Minutes before reaching the top, she realized that the tracks had stopped. The patches of snow on the trail ahead were pristine. *What? How could that even be possible?* She backtracked a bit and checked the last prints she had seen. They just stopped in the middle of nowhere and vanished without a trace. *Weird.* Heidi turned and headed back up the trail. *I'll figure it out on the way down.*

Soon, she crested the summit, pivoting around to take in a breathtaking sight: Arizona's high country, the canyon badlands, stretched out before her in a 360-degree panorama. Picture-perfect blue sky, not a cloud to be seen. *Wow!*

No people, either. Heidi had the view all to herself.

Nothing of any importance occurred that Saturday. No other hikers appeared and, aside from a few birds, there wasn't another sign of life. Heidi explored every foot of the undulating summit—the pass itself—a rectangular area roughly the size of Prescott High's football field, flanked by two rocky peaks. Like goalposts. The only anomaly was a natural small cave, more or less in the center, with an entrance protected and partly hidden by giant boulders. Empty. *A good thing too,* Heidi thought.

She spent a couple of hours resting in a comfortable spot, her back against a boulder softened by her sleeping bag, reading an adventure book cover to cover.

At midafternoon—with abundant light reaching deep into the canyon below—Heidi started back down the trail, eager to locate the boot tracks she had spotted earlier that day. To her dismay, she discovered that the thin layer of snow had melted away. Heidi kept her eyes peeled, but for what? There were no tracks—and no way to figure out where and how the men responsible for those boot prints had cut away from the trail and gone . . . where? She shook her head in frustration.

Halfway down, just after nightfall, she selected a new cove in the canyon wall, snacked on the remaining energy bars, and sacked out in her warm sleeping bag.

HEIDI AWOKE WITH A START. SOMEWHERE, A MAN HAD coughed, a hacking sound. She glanced at her wristwatch: 3:09 a.m. Jumping out of her sleeping bag, she dug her feet into her boots, pulled on her jacket, and peeked up the trail. Something glowed in the fog above, drawing closer. A soft blur wove up and down, back and forth, before cutting away from her view.

The boot prints! Whoever had made those tracks had not yet descended. So where had they been all day?

Heidi slipped back into the rocky cove, scrunching against the interior wall, staring out into the night. Shadows hurried past—not one, but two. *Of course. There were two sets of boot prints.* Men. She had the distinct impression that each carried a bulky . . . *something.* She quickly packed her gear and followed the mystery men, but no way could she catch up. Precious seconds had passed, and the fog made it impossible to hurry—too dangerous. It was obvious that the men had an easy familiarity with the trail. Heidi didn't, and now she was afraid to give herself away by clicking on her flashlight.

She hiked forward hesitantly, trying her best to make up for lost time. Once or twice, somewhere ahead, she heard the same hacking cough. Another ninety minutes passed before the canyon floor loomed below. To her surprise, she could detect no sign of the two men, not even the sound of a vehicle racing away. *How could two men just vanish into thin air?*

Taking a deep breath, Heidi dared to switch on her flashlight. No tracks. All the snow had melted under the winter sun of the previous day. *Gone without a trace.*

Heidi's treasured Mazda sports car, of course, waited for her, tucked behind the willows. But now she knew! It was true. The unknown writer had squealed on someone. But why? Something fishy was going on at Dead Man's Pass. A "crime," the anonymous tipster had written. Who were the criminals? Why were they there? Where had they come from?

And where did they go?

5

SOMETHING'S UP

The mystery searchers began calling Heidi first thing Saturday morning. All their calls went straight to voicemail. The day dragged by into the evening. By then, serious concern had set in.

"Tomorrow morning, we're heading out to Dead Man's Pass," Suzanne said forcefully.

No argument from Tom. "It isn't like Heidi to just disappear."

"Super!" Pete exclaimed. "Let's start packing. Can't wait."

His sister rolled her eyes. "We're talking seriously rugged."

Pete grinned. "That's what makes it so cool."

"Cool nothing," Kathy retorted. "Try freezing cold. That's more like it."

But early Sunday morning, during breakfast at the Jacksons', while the twins were explaining Heidi's mysterious messages of two days before, both their cellphones lit up.

On highway 87, Heidi messaged, *heading home. Meet later today. I'll call you. Heidi.*

"Thank goodness," Suzanne said.

The twins' mother, Sherri, breathed a sigh of relief. "Tell her not to do that again."

"She's one tough young lady," their father said. As Prescott's chief of police, he was a shrewd judge of people and a big fan of Heidi Hoover. He poured himself a second cup of coffee. "I wasn't too worried about her."

Sherri frowned. "Tough or not, Dead Man's Pass is a remote, dangerous place. One slip . . ."

"She's hiked it twice before," Tom reminded his parents, "with us."

"I didn't like it then," Sherri said, digging in, "and I'm not a fan now."

"I wasn't concerned about the drop-off," the Chief said, glancing over to his daughter. "Suzie, read that poem once more."

"Sure." She read the quatrain, which by now she had memorized, in a clipped voice.

The Chief sat back in his chair. "*Hmm,* a quatrain. Quite an interesting way to communicate. She traveled out there Friday night . . ."

"You know what?" Tom said. "I'll bet she didn't see anything until she ran into something—or someone—last night."

"What makes you say that?" Suzanne asked.

"Because Heidi remained out on the pass for two nights and called a meeting for today. If something had happened earlier, she'd have returned home yesterday. Heidi's got something interesting for the mystery searchers, I just know it."

The Chief nodded. "I think that's plausible."

"Oh, brother," Sherri said with a grimace. Her eyes bored

into the twins. "I haven't a clue what's going on at Dead Man's Pass, but please stay away from that place."

Suzanne's cellphone dinged with an incoming message. "It's Kathy," she said with a giggle. "Heidi texted them too. Kathy says Pete's depressed about not hiking the pass yesterday."

Gales of laughter rang out. Everyone loved Pete.

"One thing," the Chief said, turning quite serious. "Out in the badlands, you're out of my jurisdiction. I suggest you meet with Sheriff McClennan as soon as possible. Dead Man's Pass is smack dab in the center of Yavapai County."

6

AN INVITATION

At 5:00 p.m. on that blustery Sunday, the mystery searchers gathered in the restaurant that had been their favorite meeting place since junior high. It felt good to be in the warm confines of the Shake Shack.

As Kathy gazed on with a disapproving frown, Pete gorged himself on a double-double burger and fries, loaded with salt and ketchup. "You know that stuff is bad for you," she chided. "Mom wouldn't approve."

Pete ignored his sister, licking his fingers noisily.

Tom spotted movement outside as a little blue sports car turned in and parked beside the twins' Chevy. "Here comes Heidi, right on time."

Suzanne stood and headed for the front counter. The Shake Shack served Heidi's favorite hot drink. "I'll grab a big coffee for her."

The diminutive star reporter hurried inside and over to their booth, her tight black curls bouncing. She peeled off her winter jacket. "Whoa, who ordered the cold front? It's freezing out there. Hi, y'all!"

"Hi, Heidi!" they chorused back.

Suzanne called out, "I'm getting your coffee!"

"Super." Heidi, known for her rapid-fire way of speaking, rarely wasted words. "Everyone read the quatrain, right?"

"Did we ever," Kathy said. "So tell us: is it for real?"

"It sure looks that way."

"Oh, wow."

Pete was about ready to burst. "*All* of it?"

"Well, I mean you read it. Something's happening out on the pass, that's a fact. On Saturday morning, I spotted boot prints in the snow on the way up to the summit. Two people wearing good-quality hiking boots had trekked the path before me. Both of them men, judging by the size of the tracks. Since it had last snowed the day after Christmas, that meant they had hiked Dead Man's Pass about twenty-four hours earlier. That's unusual for this time of year, but it *is* a hiking trail, after all. So I didn't give it too much thought. Then, a weird thing happened: the boot prints vanished in the middle of the trail. I mean, the tracks+-+ *just stopped cold.* As if the two men had ceased to exist. I still don't know how or why."

"Had the snow melted?" Suzanne asked.

"Not quite. There were still pockets of white along the trail. I assumed, wrongly, that the tracks would continue all the way to the top. So I kept hiking. I didn't figure on them disappearing, but they did. Okay, no problem. I planned on picking them up again in the afternoon. But by then, *all* the snow had melted away. *Aargh.* That possibility hadn't crossed my mind. Without tracks, I couldn't relocate the cut-off point."

"The cut-off point?" Kathy asked, bewildered.

"The place where their trail went cold . . ."

"You mean they slipped over the edge?" Pete asked,

pulling a face. "No matter where you are on that trail, there's a sharp drop-off. I mean, we're talking lights out!"

"No!" Heidi said. "There was no sign of an accident. Or of anyone slipping or struggling to hang on to the brink—or falling off."

"Wait a minute," Suzanne said. "Slow down. Tell us *everything*."

Heidi continued. "I sacked out early Saturday evening in a cove. Just after three o'clock Sunday—this morning—I heard people on the trail making their way down. Two guys passed right by me without even realizing it. And each one of them carried *something*. I didn't have the faintest idea what they were doing, but I'll bet they're up to no good. If so, it's likely the poem's writer is correct: these guys could be nasty. One thing's definite. There *is* some kind of a 'secret run at the midnight hour.' But not *every* night."

Heidi continued her adventure story between sips of hot coffee. No one else said a word as the foursome listened in fascinated silence until she got close to the end.

Pete threw his hands up. "*Time out*! I don't get it. You're saying the bad guys were up top the whole time?"

"I didn't say that."

"Well, no. No—not exactly, you didn't. But they *had* to be. You spotted their tracks going *up* on Saturday, and then you followed the men *down* on Sunday. Right?"

Heidi tented her fingers, holding them up to her face, her elbows on the table. "Remember what it's like up top? You wouldn't guess it on the way up, but when you arrive at the summit, you discover that the pass between the two peaks up there is an area the size of a football field—a very *lumpy* football field." She paused, playing the scene back in her mind. "Lots of rocks and boulders, no trails. I spent most of Saturday exploring every square foot. Other than one little cave at the center—which was empty, I checked—there's no place to hide up there."

Tom leaned in closer. "Okay. So where'd the mystery men come from?"

Heidi drew a deep breath. Her voice dropped. "Somewhere between my cove and the summit. Right now, that's the only answer I can give you."

"Got it," Tom said. "Since they never made it to the top, locating that cut-off point in their tracks again is critical."

Heidi nodded. "For sure. Find that, and maybe we could figure out what they're up to." She glanced around with a half-smile. "Which is the reason I called this meeting."

Kathy groaned inwardly. She crossed her arms. "You're not thinking of going back there . . . *are you?*"

"You bet I am. But this time I need help. Yours, in particular. How about hiking the pass with me? We'll bunk down one night in a cove. From there, if anyone shows, we can track them."

"Game on!" Pete exclaimed, rubbing his hands together in glee. He couldn't wait.

The twins locked eyes. "We're good," Suzanne said.

"When?" Tom asked the star reporter.

"I still have two days of vacation. How about tomorrow night?"

Kathy searched for an excuse. Any excuse. "*Wait!* Tomorrow night is New Year's Eve. No way can we miss that!"

Everyone howled.

"Of course we can!" Pete blurted. "Hiking Dead Man's Pass on New Year's Eve is a dream come true."

The meeting soon ended, but not before Suzanne mentioned the Chief's advice. "We need to run our plan by Sheriff McClennan."

7

SETTING THE STAGE

Yavapai County Sheriff Steve McClennan had been in the twins' lives—and because of their friendship with the Jacksons, in the Brunellis' lives as well—since childhood. He and the Chief were the best of friends, often teaming up to fight crime.

During their high school years, the foursome had helped the Sheriff's Office solve a few mysteries. They had had the good fortune of partnering with County Detective Derek Robinson. The friendly investigator—"Call me Derek" he insisted on their first meeting—had assisted them on the Sidewinder Lane case, and the legend of Rattler Mine.

On Monday morning at 9:00 a.m. sharp, the mystery searchers—accompanied by Heidi—trooped down a long corridor and straight into Sheriff McClennan's spacious office. A large, beefy man in an immaculate khaki uniform, the sheriff stood and circled his desk, offering a giant paw to his visitors. "Hello, hello! Great to see y'all."

"Hello, Sheriff!" rang out in unison.

"It's been a while," he said, beaming. "I— Oh, I asked your favorite detective to join us. Come on in, Derek. Please, everyone, grab a seat."

A quiet, unassuming younger man of medium height, the detective stepped in, his distinctive red hair standing out like a beacon. "Hey, you guys!" He thrust out his hand in greeting. Freckles covered every inch of his visible skin. It had been quite some time since they had worked together. The group bantered back and forth for a bit.

Soon, they circled around the sheriff's enormous desk, sitting on cushioned folding chairs.

"Well, to what do we have the honor of your visit?" the sheriff asked.

Suzanne nodded to the star reporter. "It's all yours."

Heidi began by displaying the letter and envelope, which were in individual plastic sleeves. She related how the unexpected envelope had arrived at *The Daily Pilot* two days after Christmas. "Kinda blew me away. I hoped you'd check these for fingerprints. Could be few of mine and our receptionist's on them too."

"I'll take care of that," Derek said. He accepted the bags and held them up to the light. "Whoever wrote this is a well-educated individual. Female, I'd guess."

"My thought exactly," Heidi said. "And maybe smart enough not to leave her prints behind. Inside there's a quatrain, a four-line poem, as you can see." She recited the verse from memory.

A few seconds of silence ensued before Sheriff McClennan spoke. "Mysterious, but also quite revealing, isn't it? There's a crime, nighttime hikes, a 'dangerous few.' It also shows that the writer had a definite agenda, doesn't it?"

"You bet it does," Heidi replied. "She squealed on the

operation. And to *me,* of all people—rather than to law enforcement. Interesting, right?"

"Right. Did you believe it?"

"I *questioned* it. In my business, I've learned anything is possible. So I wrestled with the mysterious message for a bit before deciding to spend a couple of days and nights checking out the pass."

The sheriff leaned across his desk, pulling himself closer to the star reporter. His eyes narrowed. "You hiked out there —by *yourself?* In midwinter?"

The corners of Derek's mouth turned up. He had worked with Heidi long enough to know her capabilities.

"Yes, sir," she replied. Heidi launched into an overview of her visit to Dead Man's Pass, and her sighting of the two mystery men. "The questions are, where did they come from, and where did they go? I hiked up Friday night, crested the summit early Saturday morning. The boot tracks in the snow told me that two people had trekked up the day before, almost all the way to the top—but they seemed to have vanished into thin air."

"Which is clearly impossible, since they reappeared the next day," said Tom.

"So they were ahead of you, on the way up to the summit?" Derek asked.

"Correct. The boot prints proved they had to be still up there *somewhere,* but no way could I find them. I didn't start down until later Saturday afternoon, and by then their tracks had melted away. It occurred to me they had departed earlier —that somehow I had missed them. I spent the second night again in a carve-out alongside the trail. Early Sunday morning—right after three a.m.—I heard people hiking down. Wherever they had been hiding, it had to be somewhere between my second sleeping cove and the summit."

"But there's nothing up there," Pete objected, glancing over to the two officers. "We hiked it a few times over the years. Just rocks, hardly even a tree."

"Snakes and scorpions," Kathy added darkly.

"That's not all," Heidi said. "They had their arms wrapped around bundles of something."

Derek looked intrigued. "But you couldn't tell what?"

"Nope. Pitch-dark out there. And foggy."

"Hmmm," the sheriff said under his breath. "You sure about that? As Pete mentioned, there's nothing up there. And very few folks." He grimaced. "Especially on a winter night."

"Sheriff, I'm not positive about anything," Heidi replied earnestly. "It was dark, freezing cold, and they glided right past me. But it looked as if each one had his arms wrapped around *something*. And whatever those things were, they were all *big*."

The sheriff glanced over to his chief detective. "What do you think, Derek?"

"Somebody needs to go up there and poke around," he replied. "But I'm tied up for another week."

"We volunteer," Tom offered.

Suzanne nodded. "We're thinking tonight."

"Two days, one night," Heidi added.

"That's how you'd like to spend New Year's Eve?" The sheriff eyed the twins and chuckled again. "Your dad okay with that?"

"Uh-huh," Suzanne replied. "Mom's not a fan, but no problem with the Chief."

"You'll be on your own in the wilderness. And without cell service. You sure?"

A collective "Yes!" chorused around the room, though with nary a peep from Kathy.

Derek caught the sheriff's eye. "All right to lend them one of our new satellite phones?"

"No problem."

"You're kidding!" Pete blurted. "A satellite phone? Wow! Those things work anywhere on the planet."

"Not quite," Tom said. He was the foursome's technology guru. "A user requires a minimum eighty-percent unobstructed transmission space from the ground to the sky above for signals to be sent to the satellite and back. That could be tricky in some places on the trail, under the overhangs. No problem on the summit, of course."

Derek nodded in agreement. "That's correct. If you're down low or there's obstruction from overhanging rock, the strength of the signal would be questionable. At a minimum, you'd drop calls."

"Did Prescott High's technology club play with those things?" Suzanne asked her brother.

"We studied them, but the school wouldn't spring for any. They're pricey. You can spend a buck or two per minute just to make a call."

"That's cheap in an emergency," Kathy said. "How do they work?"

"They relay outbound calls from the ground to a satellite with an unobstructed signal," Tom explained. "The phone sends a radio signal up, and the satellite transmits the call down to a relay station on earth. Then the station routes the call to the Public Switched Telephone Network."

"How cool is that!" Pete exclaimed.

"Sometimes the call relays from one satellite to another," Derek added, "until it reaches the correct one before connecting back down to the right ground station."

"Great technology," Tom said. "The more open your view

of the sky, the better reception you'll have. Even if you're deep in a canyon, if there's a satellite above with nothing in the way, you should get a signal." He grinned. "A little luck helps too."

8

AN AMAZING DISCOVERY

And that's how Kathy, through a strange sequence of events, found herself ministering to Heidi's bleeding head wound somewhere on the trail of Dead Man's Pass. By now, she was half frozen and dead tired. Worse, Pete had disappeared back down the trail, chasing three clearly dangerous men. "Just imagine," she murmured to herself. "New Year's Eve. Oh, wait. It's past midnight. What a way to start the New Year. *Lovely.*"

But Heidi was undaunted. She insisted on continuing up the trail to find the men's hiding place. *This girl has no fear,* Kathy thought. *As if fear is alien to her.*

The closer to the top they climbed, the steeper the trail became. The two pressed onward, the beams from their flashlights barely penetrating the fog and falling snow. A thin layer of fallen snow had captured the mystery men's descending boot prints. "These tracks tell the tale," the star reporter muttered between gasps of air.

Every so often, the two paused, cut their lights, and listened. The last thing they wanted was to bump into other nightcrawlers. *Human or otherwise,* Kathy thought, trying her best not to become unglued. "You know, there're bobcats out here," she shared with Heidi, almost in passing.

"So what? They never attack people in pairs."

Minutes later, Heidi came to a dead stop. *"Wait."*

"What . . . ?"

"What?"

Heidi fell to one knee and examined the thin layer of snow. "The tracks, *look*. This is where they *begin* . . . right—here. How in the world . . . ?" She projected her light across the face of the stone wall. Yanking off one glove, she reached over and ran her hand over the smooth, weather-worn surface. "Oh wow. It's got a rounded edge here—it's like a thin curtain wall overlapping another layer of rock behind it. There's a narrow crevice at a right angle to the cliff face . . ."

Kathy edged closer. "Really?"

Heid's voice dropped to a whisper, as if she were sharing a secret. "It's so subtle, almost imperceptible. Thousands of people must have passed by it over the centuries, including us."

"You've got to be kidding!"

Heidi rose to her feet to examine the rock wall under the harsh glare of a close-up beam. "Check it out! The crevice is just wide enough to pass through! For skinny types like us, anyway!"

Heidi slipped inside a narrow hidden alcove, with a kind of partial false wall screening it from view, open to the sky above. Amazingly, it was as if Heidi was now inside the cliff and yet still outdoors at the same time. After advancing a few yards forward, she pivoted around the vertical edge of the inner wall to discover a *third* wall parallel to the first two. It was like winding back and forth through a tiny maze.

Kathy cautiously followed her friend inside.

After a brief, claustrophobic zig-zag-zig, both girls found themselves inside a small chamber, still open to the sky. In silence, they painted rays of light across the surrounding rock, which turned out to be punctuated by another opening diagonally opposite the entrance they had just squeezed through. The aperture appeared to lead to a downward-sloping path.

"What is this?" Kathy wondered. "Where are we?"

"I dunno, but we just found out where the mystery men came from. Let's go."

"*Go?* Go where?"

"Wherever this path leads us."

Where's Pete when you need him? "The others will be looking for us," Kathy said.

"Oh, well." Heidi was on a mission. Nothing would prevent her from reaching the finish line. Her light beam glided from side to side. Bordered by high stone walls on both sides, the path zigzagged in an easy downward slope, always open to the sky.

"This path is natural, it's been here forever," Kathy said. A sense of wonder and excitement overtook her, erasing her fear and fatigue.

"You got that right," Heidi said. "Those men didn't carve it out yesterday, that's for sure."

After a while, the rock walls gradually shrank down to nothing. The path continued on its steady downward slope, zigzagging back and forth in sharply angled switchbacks. The girls realized that they had in effect passed through the mountain to the other side. Here, while it was still pitch-dark under an overcast sky, there was no fog, no more falling snow.

The time for whispering had passed; the girls talked freely. "We're on the other side of Dead Man's Pass," Heidi said, "descending to—well, somewhere. We'd have a one-eighty view looking . . . must be southwest—by daylight." She stopped and slipped off her backpack. "Let's see if the satellite phone works."

"I thought Pete had it."

"He did. But he handed it to me before chasing after the bad guys. Lemme see . . . I'll just touch . . . here." Seconds later, the phone emitted a dial tone. "Woo-hoo!"

"That is super cool!" Kathy exclaimed. Somehow, being connected to the outside world obliterated her lingering trepidation.

In the distance, a faint glow lit up the horizon. "That's gotta be Prescott," Heidi declared. "Our car is down below here, somewhere."

Minutes later, the path led through a short, soaring tunnel. Emerging from it, they girls found themselves passing a maze-like array of clearly human-made walls made of rough adobe bricks on their right. Some were tumbled down, partially ruined, while others stood intact—not just walls, but abandoned dwellings, they realized. The girls swept their flashlights over every surface, peering ahead intently.

"Kathy, you know what this is?"

"Yes! It must be a village, an old Native American village. We're walking beside ancient dwellings!"

"You bet we are. Like the ones near Sedona, remember? Ceilings only four or five feet high on the ground floor, with a similar second story above. My guess is these belonged to the Sinagua people."

"Yes! They inhabited this whole area before disappearing around 1450 AD." Kathy pointed to an open doorway. "I'll light up the inside."

A small room appeared, about six or seven feet square,

with a low, blackish ceiling. "Evidence of fires from hundreds of years ago," Heidi said in a soft voice.

"Oh my gosh!" Kathy exclaimed. "This is something, I mean, big. *Really big.*"

"Yup. Too bad we weren't the first ones here. Now we know what the mystery men dragged out of here."

"*Uh-huh.* Artifacts."

"You got that right."

"That's illegal!"

"You bet it is," Heidi said grimly. "A crime, just as my anonymous admirer said. A federal crime, I think. Whoever wrote that quatrain knew exactly what she was talking about."

They hiked on, proceeding ever so slowly. The dwellings bordered a precipice that dropped straight down, much like the treacherous drop-off on the trail up to the pass. Now their flashlight beams revealed an open space to their left—a modestly scaled plaza.

"A meeting area, I bet," Heidi reckoned, "or ball courts, or maybe even a communal kitchen."

"Or a community graveyard . . ." Kathy said, slightly creeping herself out.

"In which case the guys who whacked me in the head would be gravesite robbers," said Heidi. "That's even worse than artifact theft."

The girls stopped dead in their tracks. Three wooden-handled shovels and a pickax glinted back at them, propped up against a sizeable boulder at the far end of the small plaza.

"You're right. Check it out," Kathy mouthed. "Individual mounds of dirt. Someone's been digging out here."

"Ah, yes. And they really need that pickax."

"Sure. That ground is hard as rock."

"Frozen solid," Heidi said. "I'll bet anything they dug out

entire intact pots. It's beginning to make sense. If this village site is unknown to archaeologists, and it's never been excavated or looted before, some of the artifacts you could find here would be really valuable, for sure."

"Worth how much?"

"Think in terms of thousands of dollars for each pot, even tens of thousands, on the black market."

"Whoa." Kathy cast her mind back to the Yavapai County Courthouse mystery, another case that had involved stolen indigenous artifacts. Some of the stolen items that the mystery searchers had recovered, she recalled, had been considered by the museum staff to be not just valuable but *priceless*.

The girls knelt and grabbed handfuls of cold dirt, allowing it to filter through their fingers. "This is freshly dug," Kathy noted.

Heidi glanced around. "I wonder how long they've been milking this site?"

Kathy jumped to her feet. "We've got company!" she hissed. "Hide, *quick!*"

9

TROUBLE IN PARADISE

Pete and the twins set out on a rescue mission—that's what Suzanne called it—right after the three met up at the trailhead.

"We gotta get up there," Pete urged. "I hope they're okay, but, hey . . ."

"Too bad they don't have the satellite phone with them," Tom said.

"They do!" Pete said. "I handed it over to Heidi before starting down."

Suzanne liked that. "Thank goodness."

"Any chance we'll run into any other characters on the trail?" Tom wondered out loud.

Pete chuckled. "You mean aside from Kathy and Heidi? No clue, bro. We'll find out soon enough."

The next two hours dragged by in slow motion. Pete's second hike up the trail—on the *same* night—seemed to take forever. His body ached from head to toe, and it felt as if he dragged his legs the whole way. The freezing night had turned colder; the fog and slippery snow slowed them down. That didn't bother Pete, but his thoughts did: *Where's Kathy? What happened to Heidi? Why haven't they shown up?*

Although 3:00 a.m. approached, it wasn't the twins' second trek to the top in one night. They had tons of energy, driven by concern and a certain excitement: a nighttime winter hike was a first.

"Slow down, Pete!" Tom called out. "We can't see you." The persistent fog enveloped them all the way up.

"We need to take a five-minute break," Suzanne announced a while later, "just to catch our breath." The twins dropped their backpacks on the trail and plopped down beside them.

Pete turned and found a resting spot, his back to the pass high above. "It's weird that there's no sign of them."

Suzanne gulped down some water. "Where were they when you headed down?"

"Another thirty minutes farther up, max. That's why we should have run into them by now. And quite some time ago too."

"Any chance Heidi's in worse shape than you thought?" Suzanne sounded worried.

"I doubt it. She was doing okay when I left her. Besides, she's carrying the satellite phone. She could summon help, no problem."

"So there's nothing to worry about," Tom summed up. "Let's—"

Somewhere, a distant guttural sound resonated from below them.

"Oh, my gosh," Suzanne whispered. "That was a cough. Someone's coming!"

"Follow me," Pete urged, jumping to his feet.

A minute later, all three ducked into a deep cove in the rockface and planted themselves against a back wall, looking out to the trail. Suzanne's heart raced as she worked to control her breathing, trying not to make a sound. They didn't have long to wait. Footfalls alerted them just before a tall man passed their view of the trail, heading up, both arms pumping. They waited until they felt sure that no one else was following him, then stepped out onto the trail.

"He's our ticket," Pete muttered, adjusting his backpack. "Wherever he's going, I'll bet the girls have gotta be close by. Let's go!"

HALF AN HOUR LATER, QUICK THINKING PROMPTED KATHY TO grab a shovel—*Just in case!*—before she and Heidi raced toward one of the ancient dwellings. They crouched down through the doorway and scuttled a few feet in. Whoever it was, they hoped he hadn't detected their presence.

Seconds passed before a the barely perceptible silhouette of a tall, thin man strode past the doorway. The girls crept forward, flanking the doorway, and peeked out cautiously. The man headed straight over to the shovels. He stood there for a few seconds, his back to the girls. A flashlight appeared in one hand as he stepped over to one of the nearby dwellings, bent down, and glanced inside. As his flashlight beam reflected off the snow, they could see that he wore a down jacket and jeans.

"He's wondering where his shovel went," Heidi realized out loud.

Kathy agreed. "He knows someone's been here."

"And that someone is *us*," Heidi whispered.

Racing from one dwelling to another, the man quickly

scanned inside each one, working his way closer and closer to their hiding place. Kathy tensed up, grabbing the handle of the shovel with both hands.

"I'll trip him up, you hammer him," Heidi muttered, barely mouthing the words.

Kathy, her adrenaline pumping, thought, *How do we get ourselves into these predicaments?*

They watched anxiously as the man stopped, turned, and stood ramrod straight. His flashlight went dark as he peered back along the trail before racing away. It sounded as though he had run over to one of the dwellings, one of the first ones they had passed on their way in to the village.

"What now?" Heidi whispered "He heard something."

The girls peeked out into the night. "I hear something . . . Incoming," Heidi said. "Do you—"

"Pete!" Kathy exclaimed with hushed relief as she saw the unmistakable figure of her brother, with the Jacksons right behind him, appear out of the darkness. Pete carried his flashlight with one hand, dousing almost the entire beam.

Kathy crept out of the girls' hiding place and raced out, with Heidi right behind.

Suzanne, overcome with relief, said softly, "Are we ever glad to see you two."

There was no time to waste. "Watch out!" Kathy warned. "Some guy's over there, in the fourth dwelling from the end, I think. This is an ancient Native American village."

"Is it ever!" Pete muttered back. "We followed the guy down here."

Tom spotted the shovels and instantly got the picture. "A gang of artifact thieves has been pillaging this ancient site. He's one of them."

The boys grabbed the two remaining shovels. The

mystery searchers, led by Heidi, lighting the way with her flashlight, crept warily over to the man's hiding place and surrounded the doorway, shovels raised.

"Come on out, buddy!" Tom called out bravely.

"We know you're in there!" Pete bellowed.

Nothing.

Suzanne bent down and beamed her light into the interior. "He's gone!"

"How— Where could he go?" Kathy said.

Heidi glanced inside. "Check it out. The back wall has crumbled away."

Tom lay his shovel down and slipped over to the ruined rear wall. He shone his flashlight out into the dark, raking the cliff face behind the dwelling, then returned to report to the team.

The five friends gathered in a tight circle outside the partly ruined dwelling.

"No wonder," Tom said. "Turns out there's a barely three-foot-wide ledge, like a shelf almost, running all along behind the ground-level dwellings, My guess is that it leads back to the main path to the village. Dangerous, especially at night—but navigable. One false step . . ."

Pete was all ears. "Yikes. If he had tripped, he'd be history."

"But why did he come up here anyway?" Kathy asked. "What was he looking for?"

"He wasn't looking for any-*thing*," Suzanne declared. "He was making sure that no *one* had stumbled into their secret operation. And now he knows someone has: us."

"So one of the other guys must have ordered him to come back up and check things out," Kathy said.

"Because they ran into *me* on the trail," Heidi said. She touched her head gently. "Ouch."

Suzanne locked eyes with her brother. "Shouldn't we use the satellite phone to call for reinforcements?"

"Let's not. There's gotta be hundreds of artifacts buried here. Whoever's raiding this place will be back, we can count on that. We need a game plan. This is a big deal for Arizona—maybe bigger than anything else we've ever run across."

"Okay," Suzanne said. "Let's bunk down for a few hours and grab some sleep. We can scour the village in the morning for clues. That'll be way easier in daylight."

Kathy glanced around nervously. "Is it safe?"

Pete snorted. "You bet it is. Whoever this guy is, he'll be busy blowing the whistle on us to his pals. No way is anyone coming back while we're here."

The five friends rolled out their mats and sleeping bags in two of the most intact dwellings, standing side by side, both with intact roofs. The boys took one, Heidi and the girls the other.

Pete conked out almost immediately, exhausted from his efforts. Tom quickly followed, but Heidi and the girls were too excited to drift off right away.

"Just think," Suzanne said as she nodded off. "The people who lived here probably figured this was paradise on earth..."

"Yup, safe and secure, hidden high above the badlands below. . ." Kathy said, yawning. "I get that. We might be the first ones to sleep in here since they left . . ."

"And that could've been eight hundred years ago..." Heidi finished, drifting gratefully off to sleep.

AT DAYBREAK, SCREECHING BIRDS WOKE FOUR OF THE VISITORS from a sound sleep. After a quick energy-bar breakfast, they headed out to roam around the ancient village, taking in the amazing sights.

Pete, exhausted after hiking Dead Man's Gap *twice* in one night, slept for another hour, until his sister gave him a good kick. "Wake up, sleepyhead! You're missing all the fun."

They counted fifty-four dwellings, thirty at ground level, and twenty-seven more second-floor homes overlapping their neighbors below.

"Split-level condos!" Kathy quipped.

Inside they found nothing but earthen floors and blackened ceilings,, evidence of ancient fires. "Probably to keep them warm in winter," Suzanne said with a shiver.

"And cooking too," Tom said.

Heidi bent low to enter a ground-level dwelling and squeezed inside. Even though she was the shortest one of the five, the diminutive reporter couldn't stand up straight. "They must have been a very short group of people," she said drily.

The boys spun off to follow the ancient path as it continued on past the village. Tom spotted a large, slightly round depression to their left. "What—was this a well at one time?"

"Not likely," Pete argued. "A cistern, maybe. They filled it up with rainwater or hauled water from a nearby source—or even from the badlands below. I wonder if there's another path heading down?"

"Maybe so, but *this* path ends here." Boulders stopped them from going any farther—evidence, it appeared, of an ancient landslide.

"Let's climb on top of this rockpile," Pete urged, pointing six or seven feet up the slope above the path.

"Let's not," Tom said. "It looks a little unstable."

Meanwhile, the girls counted seventeen different digs, all in the large, open space opposite the dwellings.

"It looks as if the thieves had some success here," Heidi said softly. "If they dug up vessels, that might point to a communal kitchen. Who knows?"

"Speaking of kitchens," Pete said, "I'm hungry. Let's head home."

10

SURPRISE!

That evening, the twins huddled with the Chief.

"Dad, this is huge," Tom insisted. "I mean, imagine a deserted ancient Sinagua village hidden for hundreds of years. Except for some recent looting, everything looks as if the people walked out yesterday."

The Chief nodded. "Yeah, I get it. That odd geological phenomenon you described did its job—like layers of false walls. I hiked the pass when I was a kid. Twice, I think. Over time, lots of folks have made the trek."

"But it's so remote, and a hard climb," Suzanne said. "And hardly anyone's even heard of it. I mean, at most a couple of hundred people hike out there every year."

The Chief paused for a few seconds. "That might explain why the native people built there. It's a long hike to the top. Maybe the location protected them from enemies."

"We found what looked like a cistern, but no well," Tom said. "So we figured they collected rainwater, but what happened when there wasn't much rain?"

"And food too," Suzanne added. "The ancient Arizonans

mostly grew their own food—they didn't trade for much of it. We didn't see any evidence of agriculture."

"Lots of questions," the Chief said. "Professionals will have to answer them. But I know some ancient communities farmed fields some distance from where they lived. You've stumbled into a historic site that's protected by state and federal laws. It's illegal to strip indigenous artifacts from public lands. First thing you need to do is call Sheriff McClennan."

"What about the thieves?" Tom asked. "We'll have to move fast to make sure the artifacts they've already dug up don't vanish."

"And to do that, we have to discover their identities," Suzanne added.

"Tracking them down won't be easy," the Chief said. "You're talking about the middle of nowhere."

Tom looked away, searching for ideas. "We'll work on it."

"Okay." The Chief smiled. The twins, he knew, intended on following his footsteps into law enforcement, which pleased him to no end. He enjoyed watching how every new case built their skills.

On Thursday morning, the foursome called the Sheriff's Office. The sheriff was traveling to Phoenix, but Derek Robinson agreed to a meeting after lunch.

Suzanne called Heidi. "Can you make it?"

"Sure, but I could be late."

The foursome arrived right on time. A deputy led them to a conference room where Derek waited. They quickly brought the investigator up to date.

"Good for you guys," he said. "That's quite a find."

Kathy grinned. "I said the same thing. It's just amazing."

"Does the Sheriff's Office have jurisdiction at Dead Man's Pass?" Tom asked.

"Normally, yes," Robinson replied. "But there's a twist to this one. Arizona law protects sites like this, and so does the 1979 Archaeological Resources Protection Act. It's illegal to excavate on federal or Native American land without permission, and interstate or foreign trafficking of any archaeological artifacts is strictly prohibited: a violation of U.S. federal, state, and local law—and international law too." He stopped, his eyes scanning around the room. "I promise you, these guys didn't bother getting a permit."

"So, who runs the investigation?" Suzanne asked.

"The Bureau of Land Management, with the help of the FBI. They'll both be relying on help from the Sheriff's Office as well. I'll reach out to them today."

Just then, the conference room door opened as Heidi stepped in to a chorus of hellos. She grabbed a seat and set a file folder down on the round table. "Sorry I'm late. I've got a little surprise for everyone."

"Like what?" Kathy asked eagerly.

Heidi flipped open the file folder and pushed an envelope across the table toward the detective with the tip of one fingernail. "Another letter from our friend. I haven't opened it yet. And I wore gloves while I handled it from the second it landed on my desk."

"You gotta be kidding!" Pete exclaimed.

"When did she mail it?" Suzanne asked.

"January the second. Yesterday."

Everyone craned their necks to check out the envelope. Once again, the words "World's Best Reporter" appeared under the ZIP code.

"You've got a genuine fan here, Heidi," Derek said with a half-smile.

She grinned. "Sure looks that way."

"Hang on for a sec." Derek left the room, returning shortly with a pair of white cotton gloves and a metal letter opener. Thrusting his hands into the gloves, he picked up the envelope and slit it open. A single folded sheet of paper fell out onto the conference room table. He unfolded it gently, then slid it across the table. "Go ahead, Heidi. Read it out loud, but don't touch it."

Heidi liked that. "Well, well. Another quatrain. Here we go: 'The clock is surely running down, / For the thief and his infamous cast. / Act now before they make their escape, / With a treasure trove from the ancient past.'"

11

UNFOLDING PLANS

Pete jumped to his feet. "What's with that?"

Tom chuckled. "You can't make it up. This lady's got a problem of one kind or another with the thieves. Do you think she knows we're on to them?"

Derek rocked back and forth as he considered the idea. "I don't know. But she's telling us that time is short."

"Not good," Kathy said, recalling her brother's words. "Pete might have been right. Maybe one of the thieves dumped her, and now she's seeking revenge."

Derek pursed his lips. "You're making a lot of assumptions there . . ."

"Good point," Suzanne said.

"Maybe she was in on the caper, but the thieves cut her out," Kathy suggested.

The detective grunted, then folded the single sheet of paper, slipping it back into the envelope. "Let's not jump to conclusions. I'll run this for fingerprints, but it's probably a waste of time." He pointed the letter opener toward the star reporter. "The only identifiable prints on her last letter belonged to you. Lots of prints on the envelope, of course—postal employees probably, your receptionist at the *Pilot* too, I'll bet. None that matched any criminal database."

Heidi shrugged. "Go figure."

Pete focused on the quatrain's third line, "'Act now before they make their escape.' If she's right, sounds to me like we gotta move on this—fast. She knows their plans."

"Sure doesn't sound like they'll be hanging around," Derek agreed. Like most experienced detectives, he rarely showed emotion, but a blush glowed on his freckled cheeks. The mystery searchers had seen that reaction before: Derek was in discovery mode.

"Is the stamp canceled?" Tom asked.

"It is," Heidi replied. "Dated yesterday."

"At the downtown post office again?"

"Uh-huh. That's the first thing I noticed."

"Great!" Tom said, brightening. "We might have just caught a break."

Pete directed his attention over to his best friend. "Meaning?"

"Ah," Suzanne said, catching her brother's eye. "You're talking about a security camera, aren't you?"

"Yup. There's one inside the post office. Remember, Suzie? All post offices have them. We noticed it a long time ago."

"I sure do remember."

"I've seen it too," Derek said. "And there's an outside collection box. People drive up and deposit mail from their cars. Good chance there's also a camera focused there too."

Kathy blinked. "What are the chances she dropped the letters off inside?"

"Oh, I'd say about fifty-fifty," Pete said in his snarky way.

Kathy shot her brother an icy look. "Brilliant."

Tom cut them off. "All we can do is hope. Whether she mailed the letters inside or outside, cameras should have caught her twice. Once on the twenty-sixth of December, again on January the second."

"Is there a pattern here?" Suzanne asked Derek. "She's sent two letters so far."

Kathy, never a big fan of stakeouts, suddenly realized where this was going. "You're suggesting she might return for a third time?"

"Who knows? If her responses are event driven, she could show any day." Suzanne's eyes flicked over to the detective again. "Can we get access to the post office footage?"

"Sure. Steve Robbs is the postal inspector for Prescott. I'll call him. What else?"

Pete circled back to the events at Dead Man's Pass. "The guy we followed into the village entered one of the ruined dwellings—and then vanished. After that, he *must* have made his way back down to the badlands—somehow. Plus, we know that the thieves abandoned the main trail on two occasions *before* they got down to the trailhead. So there's gotta be a secret path, one that connects the main hiking trail down the back of the mountain to the badlands. It's a path we haven't found yet, and it starts much closer to the trailhead."

"We could run a drone out there," Tom suggested. In the past, Ray Huntley, the president of Prescott High's Technology Club, had loaned drones—and a plethora of other high-tech hardware—whenever the mystery searchers needed his help. In fact, applying technology to crime sleuthing and mystery solving had been a huge winner for the foursome since their very first case. Heidi had once called it their "secret sauce."

Pete jumped at the idea. "We have time to pick up a drone today."

Tom nodded. "Okay, I'll call Ray."

The detective ran his fingers through his thick red hair. "Right now, I'm buried in criminal cases, so there's no way I can be of much help to you. If you're heading to the pass, I'd prefer you pack that satellite phone in with you—every time."

"Yes, sir," Tom said.

"Count me out too," Heidi said with a baleful look. "I'm backed up with assignments. You guys have gotta help me get this story!"

"No problem," Kathy said. "We can handle it." *Except there's no way I'm going out to the pass again,* she thought.

The meeting ended. Minutes later, Ray agreed to meet the boys at his family's ranch north of the city. "The drone? Sure, no problem. I'll be home in a few minutes."

The boys raced out to Ray's and loaded two cases, one smaller than the other, into the Chevy: one for the drone itself, one for its controller. Then they drove straight over to Pete's house. The girls helped transfer the cases into a Jeep belonging to the Brunellis' father, Joe.

Joe had agreed to lend the sleuths his Jeep, but he wasn't overjoyed. "Exactly where are you taking it?"

"Not to worry, Pop," Pete assured him. "Just a little four-wheeling in the badlands. You know, near Dead Man's Pass."

"The badlands! Holy cow. Try your best to bring it back in one piece, will you?"

"Oh, sure," Pete replied jauntily. "Of course. Never doubt us. We'll take good care of it! Nothing to worry about."

"When Pete says not to worry," Kathy whispered to Suzanne, "folks naturally get concerned."

12

A MAJOR LEAD

Friday dawned, a crisp, clear day with piercing Arizona blue skies.

Tom stared out the kitchen window. "No snow flurries today. Perfect flying weather."

County Detective Derek Robinson called the twins after breakfast. "I scheduled a meeting with the Bureau of Land Management and the FBI. Today, three p.m., and I need the four of you there."

Tom lit up. "No problem."

"Heidi too," Derek added. "I already called her."

"Anything on the USPS cameras?" Suzanne asked.

"Yes. I talked to Steve Robbs. He's expecting you anytime this morning. I'll message you his contact info."

An hour later, the foursome split into two teams. The girls grabbed the video assignment.

"I'm intrigued to see what this woman looks like," Suzanne said.

Kathy beamed. "Me too."

An ecstatic Pete said, "Great! Tom and I get to head out to the pass. It's drone time. *Woo-hoo!*"

PRESCOTT'S DOWNTOWN POST OFFICE SHARED HISTORIC SPACE with the Courthouse on Goodwin Street. After parking nearby, Suzanne and Kathy pushed through the lobby's front doors and walked past the mail drop box installed on a wall to their right.

They glanced at each other, hoping against hope for good results. A minute later, they located the upstairs office of the postal inspector and knocked.

"Enter!" someone boomed out at them.

Steve Robbs was a little guy with a big voice, friendly and professional, wearing a dress shirt, tie, and designer glasses. He sat behind his desk, all but buried behind mounds of paper. He stood and walked over to shake hands. "Which one of you is the Chief's daughter?" he asked, searching their faces.

"That would be me, sir." Suzanne smiled and held out her hand. "I'm Suzanne, and this is my best friend, Kathy."

"Call me Steve, and it's great to meet you both. I've known the Chief for twenty years. Follow me, the video is fired up for you."

They traipsed down the hall of the old building into a tiny darkened room. Before them were three chairs, a keyboard on a small desk, and a large-screen monitor attached to the wall.

"Grab a seat," Steve said. He plopped himself down in the center chair, right in front of the keyboard. The screen lit up. "Okay. I've lined up the footage for Wednesday, December the twenty-sixth. It starts at nine a.m., just as the lobby doors open on the ground floor. The camera covers the doors and the area where the mail drop occurs."

"Thank you," Kathy said. "What about the mail collection box outside? Is there a camera monitoring that one?"

"Normally. Too bad it isn't working."

Suzanne stared at him. "Seriously?"

"Yup. It's being repaired today. We didn't realize the unit had malfunctioned until Derek called. Normally, it just records away, and we rarely ever have a need to look at the footage." He shrugged. "Sorry. That's life. Now, you can roll through the footage using the keyboard arrows, push the Enter key to play. If you spot someone of interest, double-click to freeze the image and hit Control-P. You'll get a nice color print of your subject from the printer"—he opened a drawer under the desk—"right here."

The postal inspector got to his feet. "It's all yours. When you're finished with the first day, I already set it up so that your second video, for January the sixth, is queued to follow. Good luck!" He walked out and closed the door behind him.

"All right," Suzanne said. She moved into the seat in front of the keyboard. "Here's hoping our poet used the lobby mail drop. Let's roll."

Over the next hour, the girls reviewed the video from the twenty-sixth. It had been a quiet day at the post office. "Which seems reasonable," Kathy said. "I mean, c'mon. Two days after Christmas?"

The camera's angle of view captured frontal images of everyone who walked through the lobby doors. Approaching the mail slot, a few patrons angled to the right, turning their backs to the camera. The angle—and the winter gloves and mittens everyone was wearing—made it hard to gauge the size of many of the envelopes they mailed.

"Sheesh," Kathy complained.

The girls focused on women roughly between the ages of eighteen and seventy-ish who entered through the double front doors and slid envelopes into the drop box. Suzanne captured an image of each one. They had decided in advance to ignore people bringing in parcels and anyone who wasn't mailing at least one envelope. "If they're just here to buy stamps, forget them!" Kathy quipped.

As the on-screen time code clicked over to five o'clock, a uniformed postal employee appeared to wave goodbye to the last customer and lock the doors.

"Okay," Suzanne said. "How many prospects do we have?"

Kathy paged through the color printouts. "Seventeen."

"They all appear . . . normal."

"What would a person who mails accusatory quatrains look like?" Kathy teased.

"Good point. Do any of them stand out?"

". . . Not really."

Most of the women wore winter coats with high collars, scarves, and hats to protect them from the daunting weather. That made it difficult to see their faces. One lady—one of the last customers for the day—had tied an old-fashioned silk scarf over her hair. Almost all wore warm gloves and boots.

"Oh, well," Suzanne said, her voice heavy with disappointment. "Here comes day two, January the third."

Another hour passed with similar results. Little traffic, fifteen women who fit the profile, with Suzanne keying in Control-P for each one. Then at just two minutes to five o'clock, Kathy yelped. "There she is!"

"Yes!" Suzanne chimed in. "It's the lady in the scarf again!"

Suzanne backed the video up and the two leaned in closer, examining the subject frame by frame. The unknown woman—the only one who appeared on both days—wore a long deep-purple coat with an upturned fur collar that covered her neck and touched her jawline. The stylish coat was matched by high winter boots with low heels—but no gloves. And that scarf!

"We should have picked up on that before," Kathy said. "I mean, who wears a summer scarf like that in the middle of winter?"

"Someone trying to *hide her face.*"

"We can't see the letter from this view. But it's in her right hand."

"I'll go frame by frame again," Suzanne said, clicking back to the frame before the woman's right arm moved up. The girls watched as she dropped the letter into the mail slot in jerky slow motion.

"Stop!" Kathy shouted. "There's a clear shot of the envelope. Smaller than a business letter, bigger than a postcard. It's the right size!"

"It has to be her."

"That scarf is hiding her features effectively though," Kathy said. "She knows about the camera."

"That's brown hair sticking out from under her scarf. How old do you think she is?"

"Hard to say, but I'd guess mid-twenties. Watch how she moves—and look at her hands."

As Suzanne and Kathy both knew, hands can be a giveaway of age. No matter how much plastic surgery a person might have in an effort to disguise their age, there are no "facelifts" for hands . . .

"She's tall too," Suzanne said, "maybe five foot six. Slim."

"And angry," Kathy said, thinking of the messages. "You know what? If she sends Heidi a third quatrain, we might get another chance to see her face . . ."

13

SECRET ROUTES

Meanwhile, the boys raced along the gravel road on their way to Dead Man's Pass. Just before they reached the trailhead, Pete cranked the wheel left, veering off the road. As the Jeep dipped down, then up at a crazy angle, the gully with its ubiquitous bare willow trees shot by on their right.

Tom held on for dear life. "Holy crud, Pete, take it easy! You don't want to rip off the Jeep's undercarriage."

Pete grinned as he slowed down. "No kidding. Dad would ground me forever."

The boys blazed a new trail along the southwestern base of the pass. By traveling deep into the badlands and launching the drone, they hoped to locate the secret escape route used by the three mystery men who Pete followed down. And the two others who had disappeared on Heidi.

"They're able to escape with the stolen artifacts," Tom said. "They cut away from the main trail somehow and head straight down to the badlands."

Pete nodded. "Makes sense to me. After they cut down, it's not far at all."

"Exactly. I'm sure they had a vehicle waiting below. That means there must be a drivable track, one that connects to the gravel road . . . somewhere. Makes for a clean getaway."

After a bumpy journey across countless ruts and washes, the Jeep ground to a halt before a humongous gully.

"End of the road," Pete declared, stating the obvious. He cut the engine. "Notice that we're completely hidden in the landscape."

"We sure are," Tom agreed. "Can't even see the gravel road from here."

The boys unloaded the two cases from the Jeep's cargo area, both stamped FRAGILE—HANDLE WITH CARE. They unpacked a handheld controller, an extra battery, and the drone itself. Pete opened the larger case to retrieve the bird, gently setting it on top of a large, flat rock. "You forget how light this thing is."

As a team leader in Prescott High's technology club, Tom had learned to fly the aircraft in order to record school events. In the space of two years, he had emerged as the team's most experienced remote pilot. The sensitive on-board camera streamed high-def video footage to the controller's built-in screen and any connected smart wireless devices—including Pete's cellphone.

Tom fired up the controller. "Airtime is about thirty minutes. I'll watch the power indicator, but with an extra battery we've got an hour of flight time. If we need more juice, we can use the Jeep's charger. Ready?"

Pete shielded his eyes and glanced up into a cloudless, deep-blue sky. "Let 'er rip!"

With a familiar whirring sound like an angry beehive, the aircraft lifted and soared away, rapidly climbing to three hundred feet, a recommended altitude that placed the drone well above power lines, trees, buildings, and other potential obstacles.

"Even rocky summits," Tom said emphatically. "What's first?"

"The village," Pete replied. "We'll backtrack from there."

Tom maintained altitude as the bird cruised toward Dead Man's Pass, edging the red-rock rim at a fast clip. Minutes passed. *Nothing.*

"Did we fly past it?" Pete asked.

"I dunno—back we go. I'll try dropping lower."

Soon, they watched as the drone sailed high above them. Then . . .

"Check it out!" Tom shouted.

"It's the rockslide! I see it!"

As the drone paused above the target, Tom adjusted the camera angle to get a better look at deep scarring on the slope, above and to the right of the village. "See how the rockslide started much higher up? You can still see its traces, even though it might've happened centuries ago."

Pete felt like a modern-day explorer in an uncharted wilderness. *Is this fun, or what?* "Go left, toward the village."

Tom turned the bird, pushing it along a village pathway that was almost impossible to see. "Wow, it's there, we know it, but those earth tones blend into the landscape. Same for the dwellings. No one would ever have a clue that they existed."

"Crazy," Pete said. "I think that's the courtyard to the right. It fades into the red-rock colors as well."

Tom executed a three-sixty, sending the drone back to the rockslide. "I'm curious to see what's after the rockslide." He hovered over it.

"Wow, oh, wow!" Pete shouted. "Once you get past the

debris from the slide, there appears to be a route down to the badlands."

On their screens, the boys focused on a zigzagging trail lined by big rocks that must have been pushed aside hundreds of years earlier.

"They farmed down here," Tom deduced. "Right about where we're standing. That's what the Chief suggested."

Pete agreed. "They carried everything they harvested up to the village on this trail."

"Even water, I'll bet, during the dry season."

The boys strolled closer to the base of the rocky gorge.

"This might be the start of the trail right here," Pete said. "Notice how it zigs and zags right away. This is *amazing*."

In their viewfinders, the boys could see their Jeep and—nearby—themselves. "That'd be us," Pete said with a chuckle. He waved.

"Okay," Tom said. "So we've discovered how the *villagers* themselves used to get up and down the mountain. But we still have to find out how the *artifact thieves* are connecting from the lower part of the main hiking trail to the badlands below. Let's keep going. We'll start the search at ground level, near the main trailhead, but go left, as you look toward the hiking trail—around the *back* of the mountain."

"Okay. It's gotta be there somewhere," Pete muttered.

Five minutes later, he yelled out, "Stop!"

"What? What is it?"

"Hang right, just a touch."

Tom hovered, angling the drone a few degrees to the right. "Okay."

"Down, point it down. What do you see?"

". . . I—I, yeah, got it. Is it . . . ?" Tom descended, hovering the bird over a pile of debris heaped up on the badlands. "Wait a sec. Is that what I think it is?"

Pete broke into a grin. "Broken shards of pottery? Uh-huh. Looks like the thieves got careless and broke a pot or two. What a shame! Another question is, what route did they use to get a vehicle in here and pick up the loot?"

"That's easy," Tom said, sending the drone into another one-eighty. "Look what's behind the pottery shards." A twisting track, barely wide enough for a vehicle, appeared on their screens. Then he swooped down for a closer look. "Tire treads!"

Without realizing it, the boys had driven right over the same track. A minute later, the drone's camera displayed the track's intersection with the gravel road.

"That's their route in and out of the badlands," Pete said triumphantly. "Now we need to find their path up to the main trail. It's gotta be here somewhere!"

Tom guided the drone back so that it hovered over the debris pile of broken artifacts. Then he began to sweep it in ever widening arcs up the steeply rising slope on what the boys had come to think of as the "back" of the mountain. Tom kept the drone as low as possible.

Bingo.

"Whoo-hoo!" Pete shouted.

They both saw it at the same time. Here and there, scrape marks showed that boulders and smaller rocks had been pushed aside quite recently—moved a few inches in some cases, a few feet in others. The traces outlined a trail that began in a wriggling arc, rising steadily from the badlands before threading its way between a giant split rock and on to the main trail. It wasn't possible to trace every step of the way, but the overall path was clear.

"Check it out!" Pete said. "They blazed their own way. *Wow.*"

"Makes perfect sense," Tom said. "Less chance of running

into hikers—or nosey people like us. And because of the rolling landscape of the badlands, it's hard to spot a parked vehicle out here. So they drive in, park, hike up, dig, steal, hike down, drive away—"

Pete finished Tom's thought with one of the comic flourishes he was known for: "Lather, rinse, repeat!"

14

HEATING UP

That same Friday, at four o'clock sharp, a uniformed officer escorted the foursome to a large meeting room at the Sheriff's Office. Heidi had arrived minutes earlier.

"C'mon in," Derek called out. "Grab a seat. We have folks here who are eager to talk with you."

Darren Baker, Special Agent in Charge of the FBI in Phoenix, sat beside the Chief. The two men enjoyed a friendship going back a decade. The agent was a white-shirt-and-tie professional, a twenty-year veteran of the bureau who exuded confidence. Better yet, the mystery searchers and Heidi Hoover knew him well. They had all worked together on one of their strangest cases: the hunt for the elusive mastermind.

Baker stood and shook hands. "Great to see you again! It dumbfounded me when I heard about this village. Congratulations on an *amazing* discovery."

Everyone smiled as a round of greetings circled the conference room. Two other men had arrived earlier. Introductions followed.

"Harvey Weingarten is with the Bureau of Land Management," Detective Robinson said, indicating a tall, spare figure new to the five friends, bald and seemingly on the quiet, thoughtful side, who nodded.

"And Doctor Philip Meigan is a professor of archaeology at Prescott's Aztec College," Derek continued. "He's going to help us evaluate whatever's up there at Dead Man's Pass."

"It's a pleasure to meet you all," the professor said, offering his hand. He was a short man sporting a handlebar mustache and longish gray hair that fell almost to his shoulders, his face punctuated by a lopsided grin. "Believe me, I am excited to see this village. It—it surprised me, I don't mind telling you. Did you all find it together?"

Kathy pointed to the star reporter. "Heidi gets most of the credit. If it wasn't for her—"

Derek interrupted, raising a hand. "Okay, okay. Let's not get ahead of ourselves. Everyone grab a seat. We have a lot to cover. Heidi, this all began with you. Would you be kind enough to provide an overview?"

Over the next hour, Heidi—with a little help from the mystery searchers—enthralled her audience with a retelling of the week's events, beginning with the first quatrain arriving at *The Daily Pilot.* She discussed her late-night foray into Dead Man's Pass, and her discovery of the mysterious boot prints.

"What surprised me," she recalled, "is what happened the next night. I was sleeping in a cove when two men passed me on their way down."

"What time was that?" Baker asked.

"Just after three a.m. I got up and followed them, but they flat-out vanished somewhere along the trail, much closer to the trailhead. *Blew me away.*"

The Brunellis took over, describing *their* adventuresome

hike two nights later, leading to the assault on Heidi. That event, they explained, had led to an amazing discovery: the hidden entrance and its passageway to an ancient Arizonan village.

"It was obvious we weren't the first ones out there," Kathy declared. "The thieves had left shovels and a pickax propped against a boulder. We found signs of their digs too."

The boys discussed their drone survey in the badlands, the broken pottery they'd seen, and how they had found the escape path used by the artifact thieves. "Just as we thought," Tom explained, "the thieves blazed a trail for themselves, probably to avoid any exposure from unwelcome visitors. It connects the main trail on the pass down to the badlands, not far from the trailhead."

"Which explains why they whacked me," Heidi fumed. "They wanted to scare us away."

"Fat chance!" Kathy quipped.

The boys finished by describing the ancient trail they had discovered, partly blocked by a long-ago rockslide, that the villagers must have used to descend to the badlands. "We guessed that nobody's walked it since the indigenous people moved out hundreds of years ago," Pete finished.

"And then," Heidi said, "a day after our adventure up at the pass, another quatrain arrived!"

"Read it aloud if you would, please," Derek said.

"Sure." She coughed once before bringing up an image on her cellphone and beginning to read: "'The clock is surely running down, / For the thief and his infamous cast. / Act now before they make their escape, / With a treasure trove from the ancient past.'"

"One thing's for sure," Dr. Meigan said. "The writer has something against these thieves. Sarcastic too . . ."

"The verse is also a warning," Tom noted. "Time is short."

Special Agent Baker looked over to Derek, his brows arched. "No fingerprints?"

"No, but it turns out that there's recoverable DNA. She licked the seal on the envelopes."

Harvey Weingarten spoke up. "It's a 'she'? I missed that."

The Chief nodded. "Based on the handwriting, we believe the writer of both letters is the same woman."

"That's interesting," Baker said. "She seems to have an axe to grind—no obvious motivation for blowing the gang's cover."

"I think one of the thieves, maybe the ringleader, jilted her," Pete said. His sister kicked him under the table.

Suzanne reached into her purse and pulled out folded color printouts of the video stills. She passed them round. "The inside security camera at the main post office captured these images on the days corresponding to the postmarks on the letters, December twenty-sixth and January second. Unfortunately, because of the scarf and the upturned collar, it's impossible to see her face."

"But we're pretty sure she must be the writer," Kathy said. "She's the only one who posted on both days, and the size of the envelopes match the ones the *Pilot* received."

"Caucasian, probably early twenties, slender, brown hair, stylish dresser," Suzanne added. "That much we can say."

"Okay," Baker said. "Except for this woman, we don't have a clue about the artifact thieves. We need to explore that village."

"I'm all for that," Dr. Meigan said. "It's critical that my department assess the site to determine whatever is necessary to stabilize and protect it."

Harvey Weingarten chuckled. "Sounds like a Sinagua village to me. No hurry. It's already waited eight hundred years."

A frown clouded Dr. Meigan's face. He clearly took umbrage at Mr. Weingarten's words. "You're quite mistaken," the professor said. "We have to do everything possible to prevent further looting."

Tom's eyes circled the room. "We can lead a group up tomorrow morning."

"You do that," Suzanne said. "While Kathy and I plant ourselves at the post office."

15

BACK TO THE PAST

Later that night, Darren Baker called the twins at home. "Let's meet at Prescott Regional Airport tomorrow morning, nine o'clock. Let everyone know. I'll have a chopper waiting to ferry us out to the summit at Dead Man's Pass. It'll handle five passengers at a time, so we'll have to make two trips."

"No fair!" Suzanne complained to her brother after the call. "You ride in a helicopter. I park in the post office parking lot. What's with that?"

"You volunteered," Tom reminded her.

The Chief chuckled. "That's the thing about police work. It can seem unfair, and it's often boring. If you're going into law enforcement, you'd better expect that."

Tom suppressed a grin. "I'm not complaining. Who's running the investigation?"

"Well, it's a trifecta. Dead Man's Pass is on property overseen by the Bureau of Land Management. That's why Harvey Weingarten showed up at the meeting."

"He's awfully quiet," Suzanne noted.

"Smart too," the Chief responded. "But he needs help. He's worried about where the stolen artifacts have gone. That's why Darren attended."

Tom asked, "So the FBI won't be looking for evidence at the village?"

"They will, but that's more the responsibility of the Sheriff's Office. The FBI will use their sources to look for dealers of black-market Native American artifacts. All three agencies need one another."

ON SATURDAY MORNING, THE BOYS STOOD IN THE DEPARTURE lounge of Prescott's Municipal Airport gazing through gigantic plate-glass windows. In front of them, a hundred yards away, a helicopter rested on the tarmac. Its pilot circled around the aircraft, running through her pre-takeoff checklist.

"There it is!" Pete could hardly believe it. "We've never flown in one before. This is so cool."

Tom grinned. "It's going to be a lot faster getting to the village than hiking up the trail, that's for sure."

The others trickled in one by one. Harvey Weingarten walked up to the boys and shook hands. "Nice day for a chopper ride," was his only comment. He wandered off in search of coffee.

Dr. Philip Meigan arrived, accompanied by his assistant, Sam Wannamaker. Sam was a cheerful sort, even shorter than his boss, but younger and almost bald. The two archaeologists seemed rather excited to be part of the exploratory group.

"Why not?" Pete whispered to Tom. "They live for this kind of stuff."

Next came Derek Robinson, accompanied by two crime

scene technicians, each pushing a rolling evidence case. Team leader Sergeant Shannon Myer, a veteran officer with the Sheriff's Office, had brought along her assistant, Officer Cecelia Burnside.

Heidi walked up, cellphone in hand, talking to her editor. "He's curious about the breaking story," she said to the boys.

Derek overhead her. "There isn't one yet, Heidi. We can't afford to tip these guys off. They'd disappear on us."

Heidi groaned.

Darren Baker rushed up. "Sorry I'm late. Boys, you split up. One of you lead four others and hike into the village. The pilot will circle back in forty-five minutes and pick up the others. Questions?"

Heidi, annoyed that her story had just been postponed for who knows how long, sniped, "What am I, chopped liver? I'm the one who found the place."

"Go ahead," Tom said, placating their friend. "You lead the first group in. Pete and I'll follow."

Harvey Weingarten and the three officers from the Sheriff's Office boarded with Heidi. Later, the boys flew over with Darren Baker, Dr. Meigan, and Sam Wannamaker. Soon enough, all ten visitors had gathered in the village's open plaza. As the day wore on, they searched every square foot of the ancient site.

16

ACTION PLANS

That same night, right after dinner, the twins debriefed their father. "Okay," he said. "Fill me in."

"Easy for me," Suzanne replied, rolling her eyes. "Zippo. Kathy and I hung around the post office all day long. No sign of the lady with the scarf."

The Chief grunted. "I guess that's not too surprising. If she follows the pattern of her first two letters—and presuming she sends a third one—she wouldn't post until tomorrow."

"At the earliest," Suzanne said.

"What about you, Tom?"

"Nothing big. Doctor Meigan and Sam Wannamaker confirmed the village as belonging to the Sinagua people, just as everyone has guessed. Those two acted like kids in a candy store. I've never seen anyone more excited."

"Figures," Suzanne said. "So it's eight hundred years old, or even older?"

"Yup. Probably deserted at the same time as the other Sinagua villages in this region, around 1450 AD."

"Any evidence show up?" the Chief asked.

Tom shook his head. "Very little. We checked every dwelling and the village's perimeter, pathways, and open areas. We found the three shovels and the pickax, and two paper bags. Lots of boot prints, some of them ours. And the illegal excavation sites, of course."

"Paper bags? What kind?"

"Small fast-food bags, empty except for a couple of food wrappers."

The Chief whistled. "Wow. A clean crime scene. The Sheriff's Office can run DNA tests on the food wrappers, but they won't see results for some time. Did Derek bring the shovels and the pickax back on the helicopter?"

"Nope. Sergeant Meyer and Officer Burnside processed them on the spot. No fingerprints."

Suzanne wondered about Darren Baker and Mr. Weingarten. "Did they see *anything* that would help identify the thieves?"

"Not at all," Tom replied. "They asked the Sheriff's Office to monitor the gravel road to the pass. All they can do is hope that something—or *someone*—turns up."

"Checking traffic won't mean much," Suzanne stated. "Hikers go out there in daylight hours—except for a few crazy people like us!"

"That's true," the Chief said. "The Sheriff's Office doesn't have much of a presence on the badlands, either. It's in the middle of nowhere. Any other ideas?"

"Well," Tom said, "Suzy and I talked about it. We're still watching the post office, hoping that woman returns once more."

"It's a long shot," Suzanne added, glancing over to their father. "There might not be a third letter."

"There is something else," Tom said. "Remember that the

second quatrain told us the gang is wrapping up. *Not* that they've finished."

"Good point," the Chief said. "Each one of the artifacts they steal could be worth thousands of dollars. That's a huge temptation for a thief." He paused for a few seconds. "So you're counting on a return trip?"

The twins nodded. "Yes!"

ON SUNDAY MORNING, THE TWO FAMILIES ATTENDED CHURCH, gathering afterward for their customary brunch. Nobody loved Arizona's famous Mexican food more than the foursome. Over the next hour, they wolfed down hot and spicy tamales, tacos, chimichangas, enchiladas, and bean salads.

While their parents caught up with one another, the mystery searchers plotted—quietly, between bites—at the other end of the table.

"Unless we do something," Tom suggested in a firm voice, "the artifact thieves will get away. There are two things we know about them that could be helpful. One, they seem not to make a move until around midnight."

"The first quatrain told us that," Suzanne said. "And Heidi proved it."

"Right," Pete said. "What else?"

"The second quatrain told us they're still active, but close to the finish line," Tom replied.

"You think they're coming back for more" Kathy asked, her button nose twitching.

"We think so," Suzanne replied. "And the Chief agrees with us."

"So now what?" Pete asked.

"We need to be there," Tom replied. "Hiding out on the badlands. We know more or less where they park. If they show, we call for backup. When they come down with the treasure, the Sheriff's Office bags them."

Pete banged the table with a closed hand, startling their parents at the far end of the table. "Brilliant! *Let's do it.*"

Kathy groaned. "*Really?* There's no way I'm hiking out there again. It's *winter,* remember? Besides, someone's gotta watch the post office. That's boring, but warm, so I volunteer."

"Fine," her brother said. "You do that. I'm in for another jaunt to the pass."

"Sorry, Pete," Suzanne said. Although she didn't sound sorry at all. "Tom and I are going. You're on post office duty with Kathy."

"What!" His jaw dropped.

Kathy bit her lip. Her eyes darted back and forth to the twins. "When are you heading out?"

"Tonight," Tom replied.

17

A BREAK

It was past 11:00 p.m. before Suzanne edged their father's Tahoe off the gravel road, navigating her way across a ditch and onto the flatlands.

"You sure about this?" she asked as they bumped and jolted along.

"Of course. Just take it easy, we'll be fine."

The SUV lurched up and down, its headlights casting two cones of light over the badlands. A moon half shrouded by dark, threatening clouds struggled to illuminate the freezing-cold, pitch-black night.

"You turned off where Pete and I did," Tom said. "There's a ton of boulders in front of us, but we'll skirt around them."

"Can we find where the thieves parked?"

"I think so. Pete and I missed it when we were out there with the drone. But no matter what, we'll spot headlights when they drive in."

"Not when. *If*. Just saying."

"That too."

Soon enough, the Chevy reached the deep gully that had

stopped the boys on their previous trip. "Yeah, we missed it all right," Tom groaned. "That's okay. Pull a U-turn, kill your lights, and park. If they show up, we'll spot 'em."

"Assuming their headlights are on."

"Right."

The hours ticked by in slow motion. Tom played with the radio, checking sports scores. Every so often, Suzanne fired up the car and blasted the heat. The only signs of life were an inquisitive coyote slinking along in front of the Tahoe, and an owl hooting somewhere in the distance. Nighttime hid whatever else moved on the badlands. At two o'clock, snow began falling—a silent, gentle dusting that lasted an hour.

By 3:00 a.m., Suzanne figured it was a no show. She fired up the car. "That's it, we're heading home."

ON MONDAY MORNING, THE BRUNELLIS CRUISED ONTO THE post office parking lot just before opening. Pete positioned the Mustang with a view of the front doors, far enough back that no one would notice them.

"This is a stupid waste of time," he grumbled. Missing out on the stakeout in the badlands depressed him to no end.

"Says you," Kathy retorted.

"You're the one who volunteered for this useless assignment."

"Oh, well."

Hours crept by. A winter wind kicked up, and the temperature hovered near freezing. A steady flow of people parked their cars and hurried into the lobby. Everyone was bundled up.

The siblings took turns reading a book while the other kept watch. Pete left once to find coffee and returned with a double chocolate latte.

Kathy frowned. "Mom wouldn't like that. Too much sugar."

Pete slurped loudly, trying his best to annoy his sister.

Later, Suzanne called to report their progress from the night before. "Nothing. We hung out there until three. No sign of anyone."

"It's possible they already blew town," Pete said.

"Yeah. Anything's possible. Tom swears they'll be back, and we'll be there. We're going to give it another shot tonight. Anything happening at the post office?"

"Nothing yet," Kathy replied. "Not much traffic, either."

At lunchtime, the siblings pulled out a paper grocery bag, gorging on sandwiches, cookies, apples, and bananas. They settled back, again taking turns to read and watch. A steady stream of people arrived, mostly singles. The afternoon hours dragged past. And then, right after four o'clock . . .

"*Kathy!* Did you see her?"

She looked up. "See who?"

"I think our lady friend just walked through the front doors."

"Seriously?" Kathy tossed her book down and sat straight up.

"Seriously."

"Where did she park?"

"She didn't. That's how I missed her. She came from the east side of the building on foot."

"Was she wearing the scarf?"

"Yup. And the purple coat too. I figure— Here she comes!"

Kathy peered across the lot as a young woman pushed her way outside. A gust of wind made opening the door a real effort. She turned right and hurried along the sidewalk.

"Oh, my gosh. It *is* her!"

A devilish grin crossed Pete's face. "Told ya. Let's go for a stroll."

They jumped out of the Mustang, crossing to the north side of Goodwin Street, following at a safe distance. Never once did the woman glance back their way.

Kathy couldn't help herself. "So, boy genius. You were wrong, weren't you?"

No reply.

Three blocks later, the woman turned right and walked into the Prescott Public Library.

"I bet she works here!" Kathy exclaimed. "Remember what we said about her handwriting? That it must belong to a schoolteacher, or a librarian—someone who respects writing?"

Pete chortled. "Yup. Let's follow her in and browse." The siblings hurried into the multistory library, but the woman had disappeared somewhere in the bowels of the building.

Minutes passed before Kathy spotted a young woman as she exited an office at the back of the main reading room. *"That's her,"* she whispered to Pete. Kathy watched the woman as she walked up to the curved counter below a hanging INFORMATION sign. She was indeed in her mid-twenties, tall and slim, with soft brown hair that hung down to her shoulders, wearing a black skirt and a blue silk blouse. She stood in front of a keyboard, tap-tapping away.

Kathy, thinking quickly, stepped up to the counter. "Excuse me."

The woman's name tag read ALICIA MCGRUDER.

"Can I help you?"

"Hello," Kathy said, smiling warmly. "Could you tell me where I could find information on Greek mythology?"

"Sure. That would be Aisle fifty-four, on the left."

"And what about Roman epics?"

"Uh, close by, actually. Aisle fifty-seven, at the far end."

Kathy smiled again. "Thank you so much. Aisle fifty-two for Greek mythology, and fifty-four for Roman epics, right?"

The librarian looked at Kathy sympathetically. "Not exactly. Here, I'll write it down for you."

Bingo! thought Kathy.

Meanwhile, Pete—standing alone between two towering rows of bookshelves—was whispering on his cellphone. "Tom, she mailed another letter fifteen minutes ago. Get hold of the postal inspector . . . *uh,* what's his name?"

"Steve Robbs."

"Yeah, him. We gotta intercept that letter!"

18

TRAITOROUS THOUGHTS

Minutes after he received written authorization from the FBI, Steve Robbs secured the letter.

"Federal regulations," Harvey Weingarten explained with a wry smile. He had just arrived for an impromptu 4:00 p.m. meeting called by County Detective Derek Robinson. Derek, Mr. Weingarten, Heidi Hoover, Sheriff Steve McClennan, and the mystery searchers were joined by Darren Baker on a Zoom call from Phoenix. The gathering took place in a good-size conference room at the Sheriff's Office.

Derek looked over to Heidi. "A surprise this time. Instead of writing to the 'World's Greatest Reporter,' our poet wrote 'My Final Quatrain' on the outside of the envelope."

Kathy laughed. "Great! No more post office duty."

"Go ahead, Heidi," Derek instructed. "It's addressed to you. Read it aloud."

The star reporter, who had already slipped on sterile gloves provided by Derek, cleared her throat before picking up the folded sheet and reading the latest quatrain: "'The game is up and they know it, / Although they really don't care. / Unless you trip them up, / They'll play you like a lyre.'"

"Kind of a dubious rhyme there," the sheriff quipped.

A few seconds of thoughtful silence passed. "What—does *that* mean?" Kathy said. "'The game is up'—"

"'And they know it," Pete said ruefully.

"Of course they do," Suzanne said. "The thieves ran into Heidi on the main trail, and they know that we've discovered the village. The gang must have figured that we might go to the authorities."

"One thing's for sure," Heidi added. "Our poet is telling us that the artifact thieves believe they're smarter than we are. That's the reason they don't care."

Sheriff McClennan guffawed. "Excellent news in my book. Once you see arrogance like that, you can count on a criminal getting careless."

"What's a lyre exactly?" Kathy quizzed.

"An ancient Greek musical instrument, like a small harp," Darren Baker replied, his voice muffled over the call. "Only five or seven strings. So, easy to play."

"Other than the people in this room," Heidi asked, "who knows about this case?" All eyes turned toward her.

"You're suggesting someone tipped off the thieves about how far the investigation has gone?" Tom asked.

"I'm not," Heidi replied evenly, "but *she* is. After our encounters on Saturday on the trail and at the village, the gang could have been watching the site without our knowledge. One possibility is that they made you"—she wagged a finger back and forth between the twins—"staking out the badlands. How likely is that?"

"Unlikely, I would say," Suzanne replied.

"No way of telling for sure," Harvey Weingarten said.

"Not yet." His eyes shifted over to the Brunellis. "Tell us about the lady in the post office."

Pete explained how he had spotted a young woman walking into the lobby. "She matched the description. After posting a letter, she returned outside seconds later."

"Right away, I recognized her from the security videos," Kathy said. "Same color coat, identical walk, and the right age. We followed her to the library. Minutes later, she appeared at the help desk wearing a name tag: Alicia McGruder. She works there."

Derek Robinson picked up the thread. "They called the lead in to me. I ran a background check on the lady. She's single, twenty-three, employed at the library for the past two years. More interesting, Alicia McGruder is a graduate of Prescott's Aztec College."

A collective silence descended for a few seconds until Pete said, *"Uh-oh."*

"What does that mean?" his sister asked.

"She must know Doctor Philip Meigan. He's taught there forever."

"Not to mention Sam Wannamaker," Tom added.

"Could be coincidental," the sheriff growled.

Suzanne noticed that Derek Robinson's face had flushed slightly again. *Maybe,* she thought. *But that's a sign we're on to something.*

"No fingerprints on the second letter?" Darren Baker asked.

"Lots, but none that match anything in the FBI database," Derek replied. "I'm guessing there aren't any on this one, either."

"And no match for the DNA recovered from the envelopes to the FBI database?"

"Still waiting on that."

"Okay," Sheriff McClennan said. "Unfortunately, we shouldn't pull her in for questioning. Not at this stage."

"Nope. It's possible that she could alert the gang," Robinson said. "Intentionally or not. We haven't a clue about the relationships among these people. There's also another revelation."

"What's that?" Harold Weingarten asked.

Derek pointed over to Kathy, who replied, "Alicia McGruder mailed the letters. There's no doubt about that. We've got her on security video. But she didn't *write* them."

Even Darren was taken aback. "You're *sure*?"

"Yes, sir," Pete replied. "Kathy got a handwriting sample from her at the library. Not even close."

Kathy pulled a slip of paper from her jacket pocket. "Look: not only is Alicia's handwriting not elegant, it's sloppy," she said, with a mischievous grin.

"Okay," the sheriff said. "So she's fronting for the letter writer."

Tom said, "Or she just mailed the letters for someone as a favor, and knows nothing about their contents."

"How do we find out?" Suzanne asked.

"Good question. We still don't have much to go on," Derek ruminated. "I'll run background checks on the two gentlemen from Aztec College. And I suggest we put a tail on Alicia McGruder during her hours off from work. Let's see if she leads us to the letter writer."

"Do that," Weingarten said. "I also think the artifact thieves could take another shot at Dead Man's Pass. Perhaps for the last time. Someone needs to be watching out there."

"When?" Darren Baker asked.

"Tonight," Derek replied. "I'll need help."

The mystery searchers exchanged glances. "We volunteer," Pete declared. "Tom and I'll take another trip up to the village."

"And Suzanne and I will shadow Miss McGruder," Kathy offered.

Derek nodded. "We appreciate that."

Suzanne said, "Let's go!"

19

A MEETING

Suzanne found a parking place across the street from the public library.

"I checked online," Kathy said, glancing at her wristwatch. "They close at five p.m. Monday through Thursday. We should see Alicia McGruder in the next few minutes."

Sure enough. The librarian walked out through the double doors at five fifteen, bundled up against the cold, wearing her long purple coat. Derek Robinson had provided a home address just five blocks away. Suzanne left the young lady behind as she headed over to Cortez Street, just north of Gurley, and parked. Soon, their target rounded the corner and disappeared into a 1960s-style red-brick apartment building.

"Now we wait," Suzanne said.

An hour passed. Daylight faded, but there was no sign of her. Every so often, Suzanne fired up the Chevy to warm up. "It's freezing out here!"

The girls chatted. Eventually Kathy said, "You know, she could be home for the evening."

Suzanne shrugged. "You never know."

At six thirty, a Ford SUV pulled up and parked in front of the apartment block. A young woman sat waiting in the driver's seat, engine running, for a minute or two. Alicia McGruder popped out from the building and jumped into the front passenger seat. Kathy zoomed in with her cellphone and grabbed a couple quick shots of the license plate. She texted them over to Derek Robinson.

Suzanne fired up the Chevy. "Here we go!"

The Ford shot over to Whiskey Row, three blocks away. Its driver edged into a tight, angled parking spot, the only one available along the busy shopping corridor. Both casually dressed in jeans and winter jackets, the two women exited the vehicle and briskly passed a few tourist stores before ducking into an Italian restaurant.

"We've been there before," Kathy said. "Remember? A birthday dinner, I think. Great food! Even my mom liked it. Let's get a picture of the new lady."

"Okay." Suzanne circled the block twice before another parking spot opened. Soon, they were standing outside the restaurant, peering through a plate-glass window, examining a menu taped on the inside.

Suzanne murmured, "You see them?"

"Sure do." Alicia McGruder and her friend were in the far corner, sharing a laugh and perusing menus.

"How are we going to pull this off?"

"Are you hungry?"

"Yes, as a matter of fact. But I'm short on cash."

"Me too," Kathy said. "But I can scrape up enough for two bowls of minestrone soup."

"Mmm." Suzanne laughed. "Do they come with bread?"

"We can hope. There are two empty tables."

"Let's go," Suzanne whispered conspiratorially.

They snagged a table close enough to hear bits and pieces of the two women's earnest conversation, punctuated intermittently by laughter.

Choosing the moment with care, Kathy pretended to capture a picture of Suzanne but angled her cellphone unobtrusively toward Alicia McGruder's dark-haired friend.

As the evening ended, something occurred to Suzanne. "It's possible this is nothing more than two friends meeting for dinner."

"Maybe." Kathy texted the photo to Detective Robinson. "You know what? That minestrone soup was excellent."

20

WATCH AND WAIT

That Monday night, eleven thirty ticked past as the boys arrived at the gully. The ancient trail up to the village began its climb just yards away. Pete pulled a U-turn in his father's Jeep, parked, and sat back. Both seatbacks snapped into a resting position as the two relaxed and waited. In front of them lay the desolate badlands, shrouded in darkness.

"This might be their last shot," Tom suggested. "After that, the artifact thieves hit the road, I bet."

"For all we know, they've already blown town."

Fifteen minutes later, a beam of light startled Pete. "Tom! A light! *They're up there.* At the village!"

"No way! Are you *sure*?" Tom grabbed the satellite phone from his inside jacket pocket.

Pete hauled his seatback up, opened his door, and jumped out. "You bet I am!"

Tom powered up the phone. *Beep-beep-beep.* He keyed in his sister's cellphone number preceded by zero one one.

"Hello?"

"Suzy, it's me. We're parked in the badlands, directly below the village. Pete spotted a beam of light. Someone's up there!"

"Is there a vehicle on the badlands?"

"No! They must've hidden it at the trailhead or—I don't know where."

"Why would they do that?"

"Maybe they spotted us as we drove in."

"What can I do?"

"Wake up Dad, let him know. And get hold of Derek Robinson."

"Okay! No heroics, right?"

"Right." *Click.*

Meantime, Pete paced outside, staring up. "Another flashlight beam. Let's go!"

"Go? Where?"

Too late. Impetuous as always, Pete raced over to the trail and began the ascent.

"Hold on!" Tom called out. "We should wait for reinforcements."

Pete turned around. "Nothing to worry about! This could be our last chance to identify these guys."

Tom *was* worried. Still, he hurried to catch up. No way could he allow Pete to go by himself. *We're going to hear about this. Derek won't be happy. And neither will the Chief.*

It was a challenging trek—and hard to negotiate in the dark. The boys used their cellphone flashlights as sparingly as possible to find their way, dodging the random boulders that littered their way, zigzagging all the way up. Along the twenty-minute jaunt, they paused just twice to catch their breath before continuing.

As they neared the village, another powerful beam of light flashed over the ruins.

"There," Pete whispered, gulping air. "Did ya see that?"

"You bet I did!"

"When we get up to the rockslide debris, let's climb to the top, keeping low."

That made Tom nervous. "You realize how dangerous that rockpile is? It looked pretty unstable to me."

"We'll be careful. From there we can peek into the village."

"*Peek* is the operative word," Tom cautioned.

"Ten-four."

Minutes later, they cut to their right and began scaling the giant pile of boulders. As Pete braced himself on a good-size rock, it gave way under his weight. It bounced down a few feet before banging into a boulder.

Dread descended as the boys melted into the rockpile, hardly daring to breathe. Agonizing seconds ticked by. They climbed higher, ever so slowly, before poking their heads up to survey the moonlit village landscape. No movement. No sign of life. Nothing.

"What the heck?" Pete muttered. "Where'd they go?"

"No clue."

"Think they heard that rock I dislodged?"

"Well, *something* spooked them."

The boys worked up enough courage to descend onto the path on the other side of the rockpile and creep forward.

"Stay low," Pete whispered.

In the central courtyard, three shovels lay on the ground beside fresh piles of dirt. "Check it out," Tom muttered, pointing. "New digging."

Pete and Tom clung close to the ancient dwellings on

their left, scooting from shadow to shadow, glancing nervously around. They paused near the doorway to one of the more intact dwellings.

"They gotta be on their way down," Pete muttered.

A scraping sound! Tom swiveled his head to look up.

21

A PERILOUS ENCOUNTER

Two men leaped with hair-raising howls from the rooftop, knocking Tom to the ground.

Pete faked to one side before decking his attacker with a hard right to the jaw. The man fell back, slamming into his cohort and causing them both to tumble onto the frozen path with an awful thud.

"Let's go!" Tom shouted as he scrambled to his feet. They shot off, adrenaline pumping, racing toward the main trail heading up to the pass. Behind them came the sound of pounding footsteps.

"Left!" Pete called out between gasps.

Younger and fitter than their assailants, the boys soon put distance between the attackers and their prey. They hung a sharp left, just minutes now from the summit. They stopped once, just for a few seconds, bending over and gulping air. "The guy you punched," Tom gasped, forcing out the words. "You see his face?"

"Naw. Too dark."

"*Listen* . . . They're *still* following us!"

"Dang!" Pete exclaimed. "They don't give up easily, do they?"

It seemed like forever before Tom crested the last rise, with Pete close behind. "Find the cave!"

An agonizing minute passed before Pete ducked around a giant boulder. *"Here!"*

The boys vaulted headlong into the shallow underground space, where they were almost completely enclosed. There was barely enough room for two people to huddle together.

Just in time too. Voices yelled in the moonlit night outside. Pete clamped both hands over his own mouth, trying desperately to still his ragged breathing.

Tom dug into his jacket pocket for the satellite phone. He extended the antenna and pointed it skyward. Then he reached as close as he dared to the cave's entrance, touched the Call button, and prayed for a dial tone. *Beep-beep-beep.*

"Tom, wait!" Pete gasped.

"For what?"

"Don't you hear it?"

Tom paused. Then he heard it too: the unmistakable *thwop-thwop* of helicopter blades growing closer.

22

THE MYSTERY UNFOLDS

The next day, at four in the afternoon, all interested parties gathered at the Sheriff's Office downtown. No one seemed more excited than Heidi Hoover. "This is a big story—and I finally get to break it!"

"Well, you deserve to," Derek Robinson said. "Without you, we wouldn't have a case. Our thieving friends would have picked the place clean and gotten away with it too."

"And none of us would have been any wiser," Harold Weingarten said. "Speaking for the Bureau of Land Management, let me say that we owe you a debt of gratitude."

Heidi accepted the compliment. "Always happy to help the Feds." She glanced over to Derek and winked. "Not to mention the local constabulary. But the real thanks should go to whoever wrote those letters."

Darren Baker had driven up for the meeting. He found a chair beside the Chief and they both gave Heidi a thumbs up.

Dr. Philip Meigan, the professor of archaeology at Prescott's Aztec College, was visibly distressed. "I'm only sorry that Sam Wannamaker was involved in this criminal activity. It's a stain on the college's reputation, and I can only apologize for it."

"Don't beat yourself up, Doc," Sheriff Robinson commiserated. "You're not responsible for other people's actions. As the ringleader, Wannamaker is likely to serve a nice, long stretch in a federal prison."

"Good place for him," Kathy said. She caught Heidi's eye. "You were right about someone having inside information. He knew all along!"

"We ran a background check on the man," Derek informed the professor. "It came back clean."

Dr. Meigan's face colored a touch. "I—*uh,* I assume you ran one on me too?"

Derek chuckled. "Yes, sir. I'm happy to report that yours was clean as well."

Laughter rang out in the conference room, and the professor joined in with his lopsided grin.

"Who were the other two members of the gang?" asked Suzanne.

"Their names are Byron Roger Percival and John Henry Waite," the detective replied. "Here are their booking photos. They're both ex-cons, with no background in archaeology. They served as nothing more than diggers and mules." He pushed the black-and-whites across the table.

"Well, well," Heidi said, sitting straight up. A distinct look of satisfaction crossed her face. "Mr. Percival is the guy who whacked me on the head. Mind if I take this photo?"

"Sure, no problem. What for?"

"I'm going to paste his mug on the front page of the *Pilot* tomorrow morning," she said with grim determination.

Kathy giggled. "I remember the promise you made."

"Where did you pick these guys up?" Baker asked.

"Wannamaker left the village first," Derek said, "right

after he heard the boys coming up the hill. He perceived unwelcome visitors as a threat and ordered the other two to run interference." Derek stopped and shot a warning glance over to the boys.

The Chief glared as well and raised a pointed finger toward his son and Pete.

Message received, Tom thought. *More to come.*

Pete hung his head, muttering, "My bad."

Kathy noticed him surveying the group from under his lowered brow. *Your bad, my foot,* she thought.

"When Wannamaker got close to the trailhead," the detective finished, "we popped out from behind a boulder and arrested him."

"And the others?" Heidi asked.

"The helicopter's spotlight exposed them on the summit," McClennan said, picking up the story. "The Chief and I spied them as we came in for a landing. They departed rather quickly, but there was no place to hide. Derek and a few officers waited with Wannamaker at the bottom." He chuckled. "The mules seemed rather surprised to find a large welcoming committee out there."

"Boy, were we ever glad to see that helicopter," Tom said. "Those two were zoning in on us."

"Well, we nabbed all three of them," Derek said. "Thank the good Lord that you had that satellite phone. I hate to think where you'd be without it."

"We thank *you,*" the boys intoned together.

"What about those letters?" Kathy asked. "Do we know who to thank for sending them?"

The detective chuckled again. "You sent me her picture last night."

"Oh, wow," Suzanne said. "The dark-haired lady? That's great! Who is she?"

Dr. Meigan cleared his throat. "Um . . . she's Wannamaker's ex-girlfriend. They met at the college. I knew her, of course. In fact, she attended a class I teach on Native Arizonan archaeology."

Told ya! Pete mouthed to his sister.

Kathy tossed her head, refusing to even look at him.

"Her name is Constance Crawley," Derek said.

"C—Constance!" Heidi stammered. "Are you putting me on? *Connie?*"

23

HEROES

"You *know* her?" Tom asked.

Surprised by Heidi's reaction, Kathy searched her cellphone for the pictures she had taken in the restaurant, tapped on one of them, and passed the phone over. "Here's a pic from last night. She's the one with the dark hair sitting with Alicia McGruder."

"I can't believe it," Heidi murmured, shaking her head. She looked up. "Connie delivers our mail at the newspaper. We all know her. So she delivered the cryptic coded letters... that she wrote herself!"

"And she made sure to have them properly mailed, so that they'd have dated stamp cancellation marks," the sheriff added, "plus a special message to you. Think of it this way. You've made a positive impression on people at work!"

"What charges will Connie have to face?" Pete asked.

"You're kidding, right?" Suzanne replied. "She did nothing wrong. In fact, she's a hero. Without her, we wouldn't have a clue. Those thieves would have stripped the village clean."

"Great point," Dr. Meigan said, happy to latch on to some good news. He seemed to relax a little. "One of my former students is a hero. I like that."

"I'm glad to hear you say that," Derek said. "Constance Crawley and Alicia McGruder are on their way over here. I had a detective pick them up after Connie's shift. We've told the two ladies that they're *not* in trouble, but there's always a little trepidation. Let's show them our appreciation when they arrive."

Minutes later, the conference room door opened. Two nervous young women stepped in, looking rather uncomfortable. They were stunned when everyone stood, turned toward them, and applauded.

Constance recognized the professor of archaeology. "Hello, Professor Meigan," she said shyly.

"Hello, Connie. I see you paid attention in my class," he quipped.

Laughter broke out.

"I did."

Over the next hour, a lot of questions and answers flowed back and forth.

Uppermost in Suzanne's mind were the quatrains. "We referred to them as cryptic codes," she said. "Why communicate in that way? Why quatrains?"

"Oh, I've always loved literature," Connie replied, a little sheepishly. "And I felt that for Heidi, I had to make the story interesting and challenging, or she wouldn't take it seriously." She looked at Heidi. "If I hadn't done that, I wouldn't have gotten your attention. Right?"

"Right." Heidi bit back a smile. "It worked."

The sheriff wondered why Constance had blown the whistle on Sam Wannamaker. "Why take the risk that he might find out you were squealing on him? We couldn't figure that out."

"Well, I lectured him about digging up ancient relics for profit," Connie replied. "We argued, and it turned into a standoff. Sam threatened to cause big problems if I told on him. That's what he said, and it put me in a bad position. No way would I be a party to a serious crime. It wasn't an easy decision, but it was the *right* one."

"But you must have stayed in touch with him the whole time," the Chief said.

"Sort of," Constance replied. "We broke off our friendship, but he continued to call me daily. Sam's reckless. He couldn't help but leak bits of information about the digging in the village. When I learned something new, I mailed another quatrain. Or rather, Alicia did, at my request. I didn't want to appear on the security footage. The post office has had security cameras operating for years."

"I volunteered," Alicia said. "And I'm glad. We both agreed that Sam's actions were wrong. Of all people, he should have known better."

"Yes," Dr. Meigan said softly. "Just imagine: my assistant! It's embarrassing, that's for sure."

Daren Baker asked, "Do either of you ladies have any idea where the stolen relics are located?"

"I know that Sam rents a storage unit on the city's east side. He's had it for years," Connie offered. "I'd start there."

"Thank you."

"I have a question," Alicia said. "How did you get onto Connie? How did you discover she was the letter writer?"

Everyone smiled. "You led us to her," Kathy said.

"*I* did?" Alicia asked in surprise.

"Uh-huh." The girls took the two women through the

sequence of events that had led to the Italian restaurant on Whiskey Row.

"We sat opposite your table," Suzanne explained. "Kathy had taken phone photos of your license plate earlier. And of you"—she pointed to Constance—"in the restaurant."

"*That's* where I've seen you two before!" Constance exclaimed. "I've been sitting here trying to figure it out."

Derek picked up the thread. "I matched your license plate number to your driver's license, as well as the picture that Kathy captured inside the restaurant."

"We ran a background check and discovered you worked at the post office," the sheriff added.

Harold Weingarten tied it all together. "Steve produced a handwriting sample for us, some form you had filled out in your employee file. Then we knew for sure."

Another thirty minutes slipped away before the meeting broke up. Heidi was the first to slip away. Her editor had called, seeking copy for that page-one story she had promised for the next morning.

The riveting tale promised to be a winner.

INTRODUCTION TO THE TIME TRAVELERS SERIES

If you love ***The Mystery Searchers Family Book Series***, you're going to really enjoy my new series, debuting June 2023.

Just like its predecessor, ***The Time Travelers Series*** will offer great stories told with realism and featuring exciting contemporary technology.

And, of course, it will offer still more fun, wholesome, captivating, and mysterious entertainment for boys and girls from nine to fifteen years of age.

Turn the page for an excerpt from the first book in ***The Time Travelers Series.***

An Audacious Rescue: San Francisco Earthquake, 1906

CHAPTER 1

Sarah Abigail Creighton—everyone, even her mom, called her Abbie—woke up early Friday morning at the tail end of a five-day flu. She felt considerably better—almost normal. The whole time she was sick she had done nothing but drink liquids and read. In fact, she cranked through a book a day. Her parents didn't call her a bookworm for nothing. The last one she had finished was a fascinating history on the San Francisco earthquake of 1906. "So interesting," she murmured to herself.

She was getting dressed, excited to take on the new day when something clicked in her mind. *Oh boy. It's gonna happen tomorrow. Saturday morning. For sure. Mom might freak out.* And yet...

It was a Friday in June, a warm summer day on the outskirts of Los Alamos, New Mexico. The Creighton family —Abbie, her brother Jeffrey (he only answered to Jeff) and their mother, Monica—lived on an acreage west of the city. The kids' father and Monica's husband, Norbert, had died six months earlier.

Back then, Abbie had just turned fifteen. Jeff was a year and two months older. The unexpected loss of their father was a seismic shock for the siblings, of course, and devastating for their mother. Their recent move to Los Alamos hadn't helped. No immediate neighbors and, except for a handful of people at their new church, they hardly knew a soul.

Before their relocation, the Creighton family had lived on another rural property just north of Nevada's mysterious Area 51. Their father had always loved big plots of land, and Jeff knew why. At least, he *thought* he did.

"Dad likes secluded places," her brother had once confided to Abbie. "No nosey neighbors, and you can see folks coming before they even get close to your front door. Not that anyone ever comes, anyway. That matches Dad's persona bigtime. He couldn't be more secretive if he tried. *See?*"

And Abbie did, kind of.

Still, the siblings loved living in the middle of nowhere: wide-open spaces, high-desert country, purple hills and mountains, and an abundance of wildlife running over the land. No school for miles either, so they did their schoolwork online. That meant loads of free time. *What's not to like?*

Their mother, however, wasn't a fan of rural life. Monica couldn't handle the isolation and lobbied for a move. "Anywhere," she often said to her husband, "as long as it's closer to *civilization*." That meant such niceties as grocery stores, restaurants, and movie theaters.

Abbie closed her eyes for a few seconds. Since their father's death, she often replayed snippets of conversation they had had with him. Jeff called them word salads, and they usually revolved around their dad's work as a physicist. He was a civilian contractor who worked on top secret projects for the U.S. Government. That's how their parents ended up in Nevada, long before the siblings were even born.

Norbert had made the daily trip from their acreage near Rachael, Nevada (population: 70—including the Creightons) twenty-five miles south to Area 51. Everyone knew *that* as code for a secret Air Force base with the heaviest security on the face of the planet.

Not to mention seriously weird stuff, like UFO's, which fascinated Jeff to no end. "They're out there, somewhere," he often told his sister. "No doubt about it, and Dad's up to his neck in them, I just *know* it. He can't say because of his security clearance."

Over time, as the kids grew older, questions began to surface more often. Once, for example, Abbie got up enough courage to ask, "Dad, what do you do at Area 51? I mean, sure, you work on the base, but doing *what?* Our friends say it's all about space alien stuff. Is that true?"

"You've got friends?" Dad was joking, of course, although they could count the kids living nearby-ish on both hands. He smiled at her in his own pleasant way. "I'm not allowed to talk about my work, Abbie. It's a secret, but I'll tell you this much. I've never seen a space alien." Then he chuckled to himself.

It drove Jeff crazy that, although his family lived north of Area 51, they didn't have a clue what went on at the base. Even though his own father worked there! *But doing what?* Often, Jeff would throw a zinger out, just to test his dad's reaction. Abbie's brother—his parents often called him precocious when he was younger—had a generous supply of zingers ready to fly at a moment's notice. Whenever the subject of their father's work came up, he'd fire one off.

"Dad, what happens when the Air Force captures a flying saucer? What do you guys do with it?" *Zing!*

That darn near sent their father into orbit. He threw his head back, howled with laughter, and ducked the question. "Jeff, that's the funniest thing I've heard in months. Flying saucers. Wow! Where do you guys come up with that stuff?"

"Is that why we live off Extraterrestrial highway?" Abbie asked. "Because of the aliens?"

"Which aliens are you referring to?" his father replied. He

tracked a fly on the kitchen ceiling with one eye. Then he chuckled again, signaling that the conversation had ended.

Jeff claimed that their father held the world record for ducking questions.

The highway name was accurate, weirdly enough. Long before the Creighton's purchased their property, right alongside the oddly named road, the State of Nevada had renamed Route 395 making it, officially, the Extraterrestrial highway.

"That's just for the tourists," their father tut-tutted whenever the subject came up. "They flock out here in ever-greater numbers, though God alone knows why. Pay no attention to that silly name. Say, what's for lunch?"

Her brother refused to give up. "C'mon, Dad. At least tell us the *kind* of work you do."

Abbie remembered looking on, knowing exactly what Jeff had in mind. He counted on his father slipping up and revealing a secret. *Just one, please.*

"Well, I'm a physicist, Jeff. You know that. We've talked about this before. I deal with all aspects of matter and energy, ranging from basic research into the fundamental laws of nature to the practical development of devices and instruments. I bet that you might become a physicist someday too. Your computational math skills are extraordinary. Say, how's your homework coming?"

Later that same day, Jeff cornered his sister, rolled his eyes, and whispered, "Did you hear that, Abbie? *Did you?* Dad just gave us more word salad. He ducked a question for the thousandth time. None of us has a clue what he's doing out there. And that includes Mom."

True enough, Abbie thought. But if you asked her, the family had way worse stuff to deal with than their father's secretiveness.

For starters, there was the saga that had begun in the red barn. *Totally weird.*

ALSO BY BARRY FORBES

THE MYSTERY SEARCHERS BOOK SERIES

Book 1: The Mystery on Apache Canyon Drive

A small child wanders out onto a busy Arizona highway! In a hair-raising rescue, sixteen-year-old twins Tom and Suzanne Jackson save the little girl from almost certain death. Soon, the brother-and-sister team up with their best friends, Kathy and Pete Brunelli, on a perilous search for the child's mother—and her past. The mystery deepens as one case becomes two, forcing the four friends to deploy concealed technological tools along Apache Canyon Drive. The danger level ramps up with the action, and the "mystery searchers" are born.

Book 2: The Ghost in the County Courthouse

A mysterious "ghost" bypasses the security system of the Yavapai Courthouse Museum and makes off with four of the museum's most precious Native American relics. At the invitation of the museum's curator, Dr. William Wasson, the mystery searchers jump onto the case and deploy a range of technological devices to discover the ghost's secrets. If the ghost strikes again, the museum's very future is in doubt. A dangerous game of cat and mouse ensues.

Book 3: The Secrets of the Mysterious Mansion

Heidi Hoover, a good friend and a top reporter for Prescott's newspaper, *The Daily Pilot*, introduces the mystery searchers to a mysterious mansion in the forest—at midnight! The mansion is under siege from unknown "hunters." *Who are they? What are they searching for?* Good old-fashioned detective work and a couple of technological tricks ultimately reveal the truth. A desperate race ensues, but time is running out . . .

Book 4: The House on Cemetery Hill

There's a dead man walking, and it's up to the mystery searchers to figure out why. That's the challenge set by Mrs. Leslie McPherson, a successful but eccentric Prescott businesswoman. The mystery searchers team up with their favorite detective and use technology to spy on high-tech criminals at Cemetery Hill. It's a perilous game with heart-stopping moments of danger.

Book 5: The Treasure of Skull Valley

Suzanne discovers a map hidden in the pages of a classic old book at the thrift store where she works. It's titled "My Treasure Map" and leads past Skull Valley, twenty miles west of Prescott, and into the high-desert country—to an unexpected, shocking, and elusive treasure. "Please help," the note begs. The mystery searchers utilize the power and reach of the internet to trace the movement of people and events . . . *half a century earlier.*

Book 6: The Vanishing in Deception Gap

A text message to Kathy sets off a race into the unknown. "There are pirates operating out here and they're dangerous. I can't prove it but I need your help." Who sent the message? Out where? Pirates —on land! How weird is that? The mystery searchers dive in, but it might be too late. Whoever sent the message has vanished into thin air.

Book 7: The Getaway Lost in Time

A stray dog saves the twins from a dangerous predator on the hiking trail at Watson Lake. In a surprising twist, the dog leads the mystery searchers to the recent suspicious death of an elderly recluse with a mysterious past. The four young sleuths join the Sheriff's Office of Yavapai County and Heidi Hoover, the star reporter of *The Daily Pilot,* in the search for the heartless perpetrator who caused her death.

Book 8: The Hunt for the Elusive Mastermind

The mystery searchers embark on one of their strangest cases—the kidnapping of the wife of one of the city's most prominent bankers. The mystery deepens as the baffling questions emerge: Who are the kidnappers—beneath their disguises? What happened to the ransom money? It soon becomes clear that the hostage may not be the only one in danger . . .

Book 9: The Legend of Rattler Mine

In a rocky ravine north of the Flying W Dude Ranch, the mystery searchers save an unconscious man from certain death. Little do they know that they're about to step into a century-old legend that's far more dangerous than it first appears. Does Rattler Mine really exist? If it does, exactly where is it? And who is the mysterious man—or woman—willing to risk everything for it . . . *no matter the cost?*

Book 10: The Haunting of Wainrich Manor

It's the Chief's birthday party, and the Jackson/Brunelli families gather to celebrate at his favorite restaurant. Little do they know that they are about to cross paths with the charming Mrs. Roberta Robertson, who will introduce the mystery searchers to their most puzzling case yet. Someone is haunting One Wainrich Manor, a mansion abandoned for sixty years. The foursome employ the most sophisticated technology ever to discover *who* and *why.*

Book 11: The Daylight Heist on Whiskey Row

Who could ever have imagined a huge daylight heist on Prescott's famous shopping corridor, Whiskey Row? And on July 4th, of all days, just as the city's annual Frontier Days parade winds its way past Birksen Jewelers! In this captivating mystery, the old proverb

There is no honor among thieves proves to offer the key to solving a daring—and seemingly clueless—crime.

Book 12: The Cryptic Code on Dead Man's Pass

Heidi Hoover—star reporter of *The Daily Pilot* and good friend of the Mystery Searchers—opens a letter addressed to the "World's Best Reporter." Inside is an intriguing four-line poem that reads:

Search for a crime on Dead Man's Pass,

A secret run at the midnight hour.

But beware of a dangerous few,

Engaged beside the granite tower.

Wow! Who could have sent the letter? And why? Is it real—*or fake*? Time for a visit to the dangerous canyon badlands of Dead Man's Pass . . .

Don't forget to check out

www.mysterysearchers.com

You'll find a wealth of information on the website: stills and video scenes of Prescott, reviews, press releases, rewards, and more. Plus I'll update you on new releases and other news.

Questions or comments? I'd love to hear from you. My email address is:

barry@mysterysearchers.com

Are you enjoying this series? Please do me a huge favor and write a quick review. They really make a difference!

BIOGRAPHY

Barry Forbes began his writing career in 1980, eventually scripting and producing hundreds of film and video corporate presentations, winning a handful of industry awards along the way. At the same time, he served as an editorial writer for Tribune Newspapers and wrote his first two books, both non-fiction.

In 1997, he founded and served as CEO for Sales Simplicity Software, a market leader which was sold two decades later.

What next? "I always loved mystery stories and one of my favorite places to visit was Prescott, Arizona. It's situated in rugged central Arizona with tremendous locales for mysteries." In 2017, Barry merged his interest in mystery and his skills in writing, adding in a large dollop of technology. The Mystery Searchers Family Book Series was born.

Barry's wife, Linda, passed in 2019 and the series is dedicated to her. "Linda proofed the initial drafts of each book and acted as my chief advisor." The couple had been married for 49 years and had two children. A number of their fifteen grandchildren provided feedback on each book.

Contact Barry: barry@mysterysearchers.com

Made in the USA
Las Vegas, NV
31 December 2023

83746686R00075